To … sty, art-loving,
frid … d.

Best wishes
Sue

Not My Child

Susan Gillie

Published in 2021 by FeedARead.com Publishing

First Edition

A CIP catalogue record for this title is available from the British Library.

Chapter 1

Trevor fiddled with the loose button on his suit jacket. He glanced at the clock on the wall of the simple waiting room, decorated only by a vase of maroon chrysanthemums and a reproduction of Monet's Water Lilies, and saw there were still five minutes to wait. He took out his iPhone and looked through his appointments for the rest of the week – too many for comfort, too much to think about when his mind was already full of his current obsession. Where was Kate? She'd better not be late – the strain was already bad enough.

The consulting room door opened and a couple emerged. They didn't look too unhappy, not too wrung through, he thought. He realised he hadn't heard anything from the room and wondered if it was good soundproofing or whether there had been no raised voices.

As he watched them gather their coats and leave, the outer door opened and Kate came in. She gave him a quick peck on the cheek and sat down beside him. He could feel the tension between them, not the electricity which had once sent such powerful sparks, but a mixture of anger and fear. He knew how much this counselling meant to her, that she badly wanted to retrieve their relationship which had deteriorated so much and was now a nightmare for both of them. No chance, he was sure of that.

The thoughts racing through his mind were abruptly halted as the counsellor, a silver-haired woman with rimless glasses, came out and invited them into her room.

"Good afternoon, Mrs Martin, Mr Martin. I'm Elizabeth Barnes. Please sit down." She gestured to two easy chairs and took the third, facing them. "I assume you have been told the rules around confidentiality et cetera. May I call you Kate and Trevor?"

They both nodded.

"I am so glad you've both come. Kate, as you made the appointment, would you like to tell me what prompted it?" She looked at Kate, her voice calm, neutral.

Kate took a deep breath and began to speak. "We were so happy, the children – we have three boys – were great and we were so proud of them but recently Trevor seems to have withdrawn, become distant, we had rows. I began to feel we were growing apart..." Her voice began to tremble and the tears, which came all too easily these days, were clearly near the surface.

"Do you feel the same way, Trevor? How do you see things?"

Trevor was glad the question had come in time to stop Kate's tears.

"I agree things are difficult between us these days. I don't look forward to coming home any more" – this with a sideways glance at Kate – "I feel she clings to me and I resent it."

And then, unable to maintain his rational tone, the words came in an angry rush.

"Things haven't felt right for some time, not since I began travelling a lot for work. So many times when I called to see how she was, I'd get the babysitter, even quite late. I'd get home knackered, sometimes jet-lagged, and just too tired for sex – I know that's bad; Kate liked sex, but I just couldn't find the energy. Then she told me she was pregnant – it would be our third child – and I was a bit surprised, to be honest. I said so, and she got all uptight, asked what was I implying. I shut up about it, anything for a quiet life, but that nagging doubt just wouldn't go away."

He turned to Kate, sensing her nervousness, the tenseness in her body, seeing her eyes fixed on him.

"You must have known this would come up. And as young James has grown, it's become clearer and clearer that he doesn't look like me – or you – and he's quite different from our other two. He's a lovely kid and I treat him just like the others, but that suspicion ate away at me. And the older he gets, the more people remark on it. Then, a month or two ago, I was driving to a meeting, stopped at a traffic light and I saw you and James standing outside a pavement café."

Turning to the counsellor, he said, "She doesn't know this," then continued to Kate. "You were with a man I know slightly from the golf club, and suddenly I saw the likeness."

He paused for breath, feeling again the extraordinary heat which had consumed him as he had seen them standing just that bit too close together for mere acquaintanceship. As the heat receded it left him icy cold.

Kate was rigid in her chair, her eyes still glued to his face, her hands clasped tightly in her lap. The counsellor seemed to have faded from the picture; there were just the two of them in this room.

"James is not my son. You're still seeing his father. I want a divorce."

There was a moment's silence. Then her tears came in earnest.

"I'm sorry, I'm sorry," she sobbed. "I hoped you'd never know."

"But I do." He stood, took Kate firmly by the arm and moved to the door. Turning to the counsellor, he apologised: "I'm afraid we're wasting your time. What we need are lawyers."

Chapter 2

Kate pushed Trevor away from her as they emerged from the consulting rooms into the quiet, tree-lined street.

"Bastard! Cad! Coward!" She spat the words, anger and misery inextricably mingled. "How dare you tell me you have found out about James's father in front of a complete stranger. I shall never forgive you for that."

"*You* forgive *me*! That's rich. You try to make me believe for five years that James is my son, all the while seeing his real father, and you talk about forgiving me?" Trevor turned away sharply and walked towards his car, parked a few yards down the street.

Kate's first instinct was to walk in the opposite direction. Instead she followed him, gripping the car door as he opened it, forcing herself to think fast, to gain sufficient control to make a coherent plea for him to wait.

"We can't go home without agreeing how to behave, what to say to the children. They're going to notice something's very wrong. They'll want to know what it's about. Charlie and Paul are quite old enough to start speculating, and, whatever you feel about James, he believes you're his father and would be devastated if you suddenly started treating him differently."

Her voice came over not as pleading, but increasingly strongly. She knew she was right about this.

"Well?" She looked Trevor in the eye as she waited to see what he would say.

Trevor dropped his gaze and spoke coldly. “I’ll go and stay in a hotel for a few days. You can tell the boys that I’ve been called away for work until the weekend. They’re used to that. It’ll give you time to calm down. We can talk business when I come back.”

“I don’t know.” She thought quickly. “Well, OK. In any case, I’m not sure I can face you right now.” She paused. “You’ll need clean clothes for three days.”

“Pack a case for me as usual. There’s time before the boys get home.”

Kate angrily noted his assumption that she would take care of his needs but suppressed a sharp comment. It was in her interests, she decided, as she already began to plan her defence.

“I’ll see you back at the house.” She walked away, holding her head high and gritting her teeth at the thought of the time ahead. She couldn’t hold back the tears, though, and barely bothered to wipe them away, letting them build into a salty pool above her lip before reaching for a tissue. Her emotions were a jumble: shame at having been found out; fury at the humiliation in front of the counsellor; fear for the children, especially poor innocent James; and a bitter recognition that this might be the moment when the full story might come out, and that this was a make-or-break point in their marriage, a marriage that she didn’t want to break. Indeed, she had spent the past five years ensuring – she had thought – that it wouldn’t. She was certain that, in spite of everything, she didn’t want to lose Trevor. For all his faults, his past and present behaviour, she knew he was fundamentally a good and kind man, husband, father and provider. She was fond of him – no, damn it, she loved him.

Finding her way back to her own car, she drove as if on autopilot to their substantial Edwardian house set back from the leafy Redland street, close to the Bristol Downs where they had spent so many happy times with the children, cycling, flying kites, picnicking. “Not much equity to share there,” she thought to herself grimly as she turned into the gravelled drive, remembering her qualms at the size of the mortgage when they bought the house.

Trevor was already in the house, going through papers in his study. He didn't look up as she went past the door and up to their room. She accepted his silence and rapidly put three days' necessities into a suitcase, carried it downstairs and put it outside the study door.

"Here you are. You'd better go quickly before the boys get home. I can't face them with you in the house."

Trevor glanced at her, his face impassive, put a pile of papers into his briefcase, closed it and stood up. "I'll come back Saturday morning," he muttered, "and take them to football before lunch as usual. We can probably manage a civil front for a few hours until they're in bed. Then we can talk." Kate nodded agreement. He picked up the case and walked to the front door. "You can text me if you absolutely have to." And he was gone.

Suddenly exhausted, Kate slumped into a chair in the kitchen and sat there, staring numbly into space. After a few minutes, she roused herself sufficiently to put the kettle on and make a cup of tea which she drank slowly, reluctant to think about anything except the imminent arrival of the children. How fortunate that it was not her day for fetching them, and that Ann, whose turn it was, would not want to stop for a chat.

She wasn't sure how she got through that afternoon and evening. She explained to the boys that Daddy wouldn't be home to read to them as he was away on unexpected business until the weekend. She compensated by allowing second helpings of ice cream with their supper and a longer bath time than usual. She read a bedtime story to little James while the older two played in their room until it was their turn – at eight and ten they still loved being tucked into bed and read to before some quiet talking time on their own.

"Lights out," Kate called up the stairs, hoping that for once they wouldn't complain. To her relief, all was soon quiet and she was able to collapse on the sofa and force her mind to serious thought about how she could save her marriage.

Chapter 3

Over the next three days Kate performed her daily tasks mechanically, loading and emptying the washing machine and dishwasher, ironing a few blouses, checking her emails. She was perversely glad the cleaning lady was on holiday; she couldn't face making polite conversation over cups of tea.

Determinedly, she concentrated on the boys before and after school, asking about their days and their friends, helping with homework. She called Ann, an old friend as well as school run sharer, to enlist her help on the Saturday, but otherwise she stayed at home alone, living in her head, her mind racing through possibility and counter-possibility, holding imaginary conversations with Trevor. Occasionally tears came unbidden as her thoughts strayed into the possible failure of their marriage. Sometimes, though, she allowed herself a secret smile as she imagined Trevor's discomfort when she brought out the whole story.

Saturday came, and the boys, excited at the thought of their father's return, were full of energy, their bounce almost unbearable to Kate, who longed for them to be off to their football sessions. At ten she heard the key turn in the lock, and there was Trevor, looking grim and tired, his suit rumpled. He dropped his case on the hall floor.

"Hi boys," he smiled and briefly looked better, though he barely glanced at her. He gave each of them a hug. "Ready?" The boys hung around him while she fetched their kit.

The phone rang, a shock in the tense atmosphere, and Trevor answered it immediately. "Yes, of course, what a good idea, they'd love it... No, no hurry, we'll fetch them at bedtime."

Kate raised an eyebrow as he hung up.

"That was Ann. She wants all three to go to their house after football for lunch, a children's theatre outing and a barbeque – how convenient." There was a sarcastic edge to his tone.

Kate nodded. The butterflies in her stomach fluttered wildly; she knew there was no going back if she wanted to save the marriage.

"Be good! Have fun and tell me all about it later." She kissed the boys goodbye, waving as they followed Trevor to his car, the three of them like Russian dolls in their decreasing size. They seemed a little subdued now, not surprising, she thought; they must have picked up something of the tension in the air. Her heart hammered; if she didn't succeed, this might be the end of their family. How they would break the news, how would they take it, especially James? She mustn't fail.

She set the scrubbed pine kitchen table for lunch and prepared the Italian salads she knew Trevor loved. She took the meats and cheeses out of the refrigerator to allow their aroma to fill the kitchen and selected a loaf from the freezer to be heated and add its inimitable, heady smell just before he returned.

Going up to their room, she ran a hot bath, adding plenty of her favourite lavender essence, and willed herself to relax as the steam rose and misted the mirror. It was not hard to remember the many happy times they had spent together: the excitement of setting up their first home; the amazement and mutual joy as their first son was born; holidays on sandy beaches, laughing as they raced into the chilly waters of the English coast; lazy evenings at home cuddled on the sofa watching the old movies they both loved. However, thinking back further to when they had first met produced a blush, even now after so many years, as she remembered what an unpropitious occasion that had been.

She and a group of fellow students had been celebrating Ann's birthday. Admiring the view over Bristol from the little balcony of Ann's flat on the top floor of a small block in hilly Clifton, wine glass in hand, she had turned to watch the setting sun and knocked over her open bag lying at her feet. As luck had it, her keys were on top; they slipped out and, before she could stop them, slid under the protective railings and fell down to the garden of a house in the street below, to be followed by a shout of, "Christ, is someone trying to murder me?"

She looked down and saw the dark head of a young man looking up, clutching the side of his neck where, even from that height, blood could be seen staining the side of his white collar.

"Good God, what do you think you're doing?" he shouted up. "You could bloody well have killed me."

"Oh, heavens, I'm really, really sorry. Honestly, it was a stupid accident – I just knocked my bag over and the keys fell out..."

"Well, be more fucking careful next time."

Embarrassed as she was, she hardly dared ask: "Sorry again, but could you give me a few minutes as I'll have to come down to get them. Or I can meet you in the street in front of this block, number 25. Might be better. That OK?"

"All right. Number 25 – five minutes." He did not sound pleased.

"I don't know what to say except sorry," she mumbled, barely able to meet his eye as they met outside the house and taking the proffered keys. "But, please, do come up and let me wash the cut and put a plaster on it."

The young man nodded and followed her up the stairs. The blood stain was considerable by then and her friends' eyes widened as he came into the flat. Ann produced sticking plasters, and Kate led him into the bathroom, apologising profusely all the time, secretly worried that the wound was actually serious.

"I'm Kate Adamson, by the way," she eventually volunteered as she lifted his shirt off gently and reached for some cotton wool to clean the wound which, to her relief, was only seeping blood now, and was not as large as she had first feared. "What's your name?"

"Trevor. Trevor Martin." He winced as, reaching up, she cleaned the blood away. "Do you live here?"

"No, this is Ann's flat. We were just having a birthday drink – we're all second-year students. You?"

"Me too, a student, I mean; law, final year. Ouch."

As she continued cleaning the wound, she relaxed a little and took stock of the tall, slim young man in front of her. His hair was dark and just a little wavy, his skin smooth and lightly tanned, and there was just enough definition in his chest muscles to suggest fitness. In spite of herself she began to see him as someone she would like to know in happier circumstances. Apologising yet again for the stain and tear in the shirt, she helped him back into it and led him into the living room where her friends were still drinking.

Ann – the same Ann who had been her bridesmaid, who still lived in Bristol and whose help she had enlisted this afternoon – came forward and offered him a glass of wine which he accepted, and then a second. As he relaxed he proved a good conversationalist, his mood improved and they started to chat. He was funny as well as very intelligent, and she quickly stopped noticing that his speech was not as polished as her friends'; there was just a touch of what her parents called 'Sarf London', softened by the hint of a Somerset burr.

As he left he smiled and his eyes held a slight twinkle: "How about buying me a compensatory drink, then maybe, just maybe, I shall forgive you. Early evening tomorrow, say 6.30? That boat restaurant on Welsh Back. Know it?"

Surprised but pleased, Kate accepted shyly, hoping she wasn't blushing. When he had left, she giggled over the incident with Ann and the others.

"You must tell us how it goes," they laughed. "He's pretty dishy!"

"OK, but don't expect too much; I think he was pretty pissed off about his shirt, even though he didn't say anything."

Next evening Kate washed her long blond hair, applied lipstick and flattering touches of blusher. She had bought a new white shirt of the correct size, noted the day before, and went to the rendezvous clutching it somewhat nervously.

He was waiting when she arrived. Once they were seated at a table overlooking the water, she handed over the parcel.

"Sorry again! I checked the size when you took it off, so it should fit." She was sure this time she did blush.

"That's kind of you; you didn't have to. It was only an old shirt." He was clearly surprised, even a little embarrassed, and touched at her gift. He unwrapped it and agreed it was indeed the right size. Conversation flowed easily and they touched on many subjects, not just comparing their experience of the university and her history course, but politics and cycling on Bristol's busy – and hilly – roads.

Kate glanced at her watch. "Good heavens! Talking of cycling and hilly roads, look at the time and I've got to cycle back up to Clifton. Where do you live?"

"The other side of town, not so grand. I was visiting a friend last night." He smiled a little apologetically. "Shall we do this again?" He looked at her hopefully.

"Yes let's." She didn't attempt to hide her pleasure, picked up a clean paper napkin and wrote her phone number on it. He tore off a corner, wrote his and passed it to her.

They parted a little shyly, not sure if even a peck on the cheek would be welcome, but things progressed rapidly from that meeting: another evening drink, student parties, a walk along the Avon interrupted by frequent stops for kisses and, before long, sex became a frequent event. Both were veterans of casual student affairs, but now learnt the pleasure of making love with someone who really cared.

That year she had viewed the end of term with very mixed feelings. She always enjoyed the return home: her parents, though respecting her increasing independence, were patently thrilled to have her, their younger daughter, back home. The family's two Labradors, overexcited at seeing her, were in danger of smothering her with slobbery kisses. The big Georgian house in a leafy Buckinghamshire village was almost a cliché of The Old Rectory and was full of memories as well as the lovely furniture her parents had inherited or collected over the years. In midsummer the garden, too, was a delight, with her father's beloved vegetable beds burgeoning with early produce, and her mother's wide herbaceous borders wondrously full of colour.

However, parting from Trevor had been hard.

"When shall I see you again? What are you doing for the summer?" she asked as they lay side by side in the grass on the Downs in the warm June sunshine, looking up at the few cotton wool clouds floating above them.

"I'm not sure yet," he replied. "You know I'd love to be in Bristol with you, but I may take up the offer I got of a placement in a top firm of solicitors in London. That's quite a coup, placements are really hard to get and I'd have to start in a couple of weeks. But, I don't know, I might come back to Bristol to do a Masters, might help getting even better jobs."

"Promise you'll tell me as soon as you've decided? And anyway, if you're in London, you could come and visit me at home. It's not far and it's lovely there – and you'd get on really well with my parents – and the dogs!"

"Mmm, I'm not sure. But I will write and call, I promise!"

She thought about suggesting she visit him instead, but he had never really talked about his family, and his reticence held her back.

Next day he saw her off at the station. They held one another close for a long minute before Kate went through the barrier and down to the London platform. As she emerged into the daylight, she saw he was still there. He waved and blew her a kiss. A warm wave of happiness swept over her as she was sure she saw him mouth "I love you."

Her heart leapt when she soon found a postcard from him on the Old Rectory doormat. She wasted no time in looking at the picture but turned it over to read:

Dear Kate. I have decided to do the Masters. We shall be together again in the autumn. xx and a big hug, love Trevor.

She rang Trevor in delight, the first of many calls, the privacy of her room or the garden allowing uninhibited exchanges. When it was time to return to Bristol, she gave him the day and train. He was there at the station barrier and, pausing only long enough to take her suitcase from her, he enveloped her in a bear hug, before kissing her deeply. "I am so very, very happy to see you," he whispered in her ear. "I didn't tell you before, but I decided to do the Masters so we could be together."

It had become clear that this was no passing romance. A smile of remembrance flickered as Kate recalled their continuing courtship, and her pleasure in discovering that Trevor had a strong romantic streak: he would greet her with a posy of wildflowers he had picked, or produce a candle to grace the table of the cheap restaurant where they sometimes met. And of course, he had gone down on one knee to ask her to marry him at the end of her final year.

A shiver induced by the cooling bathwater returned her to the present and the difficult time ahead, and she reluctantly stepped out of the bath to continue her preparations.

With newly washed hair, careful but discreet make-up, and wearing a pretty sweater and skirt, she didn't need a mirror to know she looked really good: tall and slim, clearly still young enough to wear her hair long and straight. She lifted the short skirt a little and smiled to herself as she revealed her shapely legs in stockings held up by lacy suspenders – she knew he couldn't resist them, and she would be careful to allow him the occasional, accidental glimpse. All's fair, she thought.

Chapter 4

It was nearly one o'clock by the time Trevor returned from handing the three boys over to Ann after watching them at football. As he entered the hall, he was assailed by the delicious smells of warm bread and pungent cheeses emanating from the kitchen.

They were warily polite with each other as Kate put the finishing touches to the table.

"Please could you put out clean napkins from the dresser, oh and the wine glasses. And pepper and salt if you think we'll need them."

The small tasks eased the tension. Trevor actually smiled as, by telepathic agreement, they sat down to eat. It was a silent feast, but a good one. She had opened a bottle of Chianti and, her nerves slightly calmed by a glass or two, she ventured, "Well, it was this or kid's food, and I know you like Italian."

He nodded. "It's good. Hotel food is all very well in its way, but you never get this freshly prepared feel; the aromas are lost by the time the food gets to the table."

"How did the boys get on at football? Did you have all the clean clothes they needed?"

"They enjoyed it as usual. It was training then short games. Ann's boys were happy to see them."

However, the strain of the situation hung over them both and they mostly ate in silence.

Kate soon stood up. "I'll make coffee and then we can talk."

The butterflies in her stomach were enormous but Kate managed to pour the coffee and carry the tray with the cups and sugar without spilling to join Trevor in the sitting room. They sat in the enveloping chintzy armchairs either side of the fireplace. A moment's silence ensued, both of them horribly aware of what was about to be said.

Taking a deep breath, Kate looked directly at Trevor and began.

"You are right, James is not your son. His father, as you realised, is Jonathan Markham, but no, I am not still 'seeing him' in the way you implied. I feel terrible about the deception – I truly wish I had come clean about everything before, but I was angry, confused and scared..."

"Angry?" Trevor, who had looked cold and mulish suddenly responded sharply.

"Yes, angry." She took another deep breath, preparing for the shock she knew this would be, and that it might backfire, but she had to do it. "We were so happy at the beginning, with Charlie and Paul, your job going well, money worries receding – we didn't have to count the pennies any more. I looked forward to your coming home in the evenings, how we felt like a real family, what fun we had at weekends." She could feel that glow, the sense of love and security which had enveloped her in those days. It made it easier to go on.

"Then you began to work longer hours, got promotion, started travelling. It was tough then, but I didn't complain. I tried to keep busy and occupy my mind with evening classes – we could afford babysitters by then – and seeing my friends." She looked up at him. He nodded.

"It got worse. Sometimes you didn't get home until I was in bed, even asleep. I would call you at the office and not get through. When you were away, you never seemed to be in your hotel room. Sometimes, when I rang, I got Nicola, your assistant – you remember Nicola?" Again, she looked at him, pointedly this time, and held his eye. She knew him so well she could sense a slight tensing and pushed on.

"Remember her? The leggy one with big boobs, too-short skirts and loads of mascara?" She stopped just short of crudeness, though she wanted to say a lot more.

Trevor nodded. "Nicola Johnson, she worked for me for a couple of years. Good brain, but a bit scatty."

"Well, she's Nicola Bryant now." Trevor looked at her quickly, but she didn't pause long enough for him to ask how she knew or why she brought it up. "This scatty Nicola started to get a bit odd on the phone, sort of proprietary about you, and aggressive, and I didn't like it.

"Then at the office Christmas party six years ago I watched her dancing with you and..." She swallowed hard, remembering the shock at seeing them holding each other so closely, the horrible realisation that it was more than a professional relationship she was witnessing. "It was awful. I felt such a fool. I wondered who in the office knew, whether they were all looking at me and nudging each other, talking about me. I don't know how I kept going that evening, but I made a decision not to say anything unless you did – I know office romances come and go, and I just hoped it would fade away quickly."

He was blushing now, something she had never seen before. "You knew? And said nothing?" She was silent. "But," he blustered, "you were right, it did pass. I got rid of her soon after..."

"Not soon enough – but I'll get to that." She gritted her teeth and carried on. "I don't know how I coped that Christmas. I kept cheerful for the sake of Charlie and Paul, tried not to behave differently towards you." Tears came to her eyes as she remembered how hard it had been not to blurt everything out, how miserably she had subjected herself to his rather drunken embraces over the holiday, and the relief she had felt when he went back to work for the last few days of the year.

She knocked the spoon off her saucer and slid forward in her chair to pick it up, carefully allowing her skirt to ride up as she did so. She saw his eyes flick towards her legs. She sat up again and paused for a second.

"We had tickets for the New Year's Eve party at the golf club. You rang at teatime from the office to say you'd be a bit late as you had work to finish. Then you rang again at half past seven saying I should go on and you'd meet me there. So I did, and you didn't come. Remember?"

Trevor inclined his head, his eyes downcast; she could feel his embarrassment.

"I felt so conspicuous, so stupid making your excuses to everyone. It was awful; it hurt so much as I could guess where you were – or rather who you were with. What humiliation.

"I decided to brazen it out, not run home, but of course I drank too much. When midnight came and I was alone among all those couples, I thought I would die. But Jonathan came up to me, and gave me a hug and a kiss, and said nice things, that a woman like me shouldn't be on her own on New Year's Eve. Then I began to worry about how I was going to get home – I wasn't fit to drive – and Jonathan came up again and said, could he give me a lift as his wife wasn't feeling well and had gone home in a taxi. Of course, I said yes.

"Do I have to go on?" She looked pleadingly at him.

He shook his head; she knew he understood and didn't want to know the details. She sensed his guilt was stronger now than it had been then.

"When I got home, you were asleep so I showered and went to bed in the spare room. I felt dirty and ashamed – but still angry and humiliated. I couldn't face waking up beside you. Next morning we had a blazing row, our first ever – the boys hated it – but I still kept quiet about bloody Nicola. After all, now I had a dirty secret too."

He opened his mouth to speak, but she held up her hand to stop him. "Let me finish, I've not done yet. So, you must remember how we kept going then, with you working late, travelling a lot, exhausted; me still suspecting you were seeing Nicola, feeling so confused but still hoping that we could come to a happy ending. I really, really worked at keeping us together.

"Then came the next shock; I found I was pregnant. We'd made love so seldom those past months that I knew there had to be a chance it was Jonathan's, but I hoped against hope that I was wrong, that it was your baby – I convinced myself that it had to be – so I just didn't say anything, and when you were surprised and got suspicious I just denied any other possibility. I thought once the baby arrived, all would be well again, and it was, for a long time. Your workload lessened – or you stopped seeing Nicola – and we got back to nearly normal. I stopped being concerned and felt we were a happy family again. I didn't realise your doubts were forming again, but of course it was obvious that something was going very wrong these past few months. That's why I suggested the counsellor."

He opened his mouth to speak but again she rushed on:

"There's something I must say before we go any further: I love you and I don't want us to divorce. I can't bear the thought of the family split apart, the pain and heartache, the effect on the boys. James loves you as his father, and if he'd looked like me you'd never have known any different. Think how he'd feel if he knew he was the cause of the family breaking up."

Trevor was almost on his feet with impatience and speaking before she finished.

"But what about Jonathan? I saw you standing so close together, looking so intimate. It's obvious he knows. How can you say you're not seeing him? How can he face me at the golf club? This is unbelievable." He thumped his fist on the arm of his chair.

Kate forced herself to stay calm and speak steadily.

"I told Jonathan when I realised for sure he was James's father, when I couldn't deny it to myself any longer. I thought he might notice – not that our paths cross that often – and I wanted him to know that I didn't want anything from him. We both knew there was nothing between us; that night had been just one of those stupid, drunken things which we both regretted – yes, him as much as me – and which we'd have preferred to forget. But once I'd told him, he was amazing; he just said I could talk to him whenever I needed to, that he didn't want to put any strain on either marriage, that though it was nice to see James growing into such a fine boy, he wouldn't dream of becoming a presence in his life. That time you saw us together was when I had called him to say I desperately needed to talk about how hard things were at home, and how I hoped it wasn't about James."

They both sat silent for a few moments. She felt wrung through, but she knew there was one more revelation to make, the one she hoped would be the deciding factor, but she held back.

Chapter 5

"Why don't you tell me your side of the story? How long did your thing with Nicola go on for? When did you stop seeing her? What do you have to say for yourself?" Kate couldn't stop a note of bitterness creeping in.

Trevor looked out of the window as he spoke, unable to meet Kate's eye.

"It began like so many office affairs: late working, poring over documents together, that chemistry thing building up. She had a way of looking into my eyes as she spoke, gave me the impression she thought I was special. It's hard to resist that, and that spark when our hands touched as we went through contracts together.

"We started having a drink after work, I suppose about a year before that Christmas party, then she was sent to accompany me on a business trip to Germany. We had dinner together, as one does on a trip like that, and I can't deny she was making it clear she fancied me, and of course I found it flattering. A bottle of wine between us was enough to lower my resistance and that was when it really began.

"She was good company – not that you're not! – and you're right, she doesn't have your class – or your legs," this with a disarming grin and a glance towards Kate's stocking tops, still just visible beneath her skirt.

"And I found the complicity, the planning and secrecy very exciting – it was almost too easy, sometimes, to invent the need to work late. It got more and more frequent – and I was often exhausted by the double life, as you noticed. But after that New Year's Day row, I did begin to wonder what I was doing, whether I had pushed my luck too far. I don't think I ever really thought I was in love with her – it was a sex thing. I certainly didn't have any intention of breaking our marriage for her.

"But then I began to realise that she had long term designs on me, and I couldn't cope with that. Our meetings got more and more intense; she would start to describe the life we could have together, and I'd try to convince her to stop, that it was pointless.

"In the end, it was becoming embarrassing; I couldn't cope with her demands for more and more time when I knew you were pregnant and needed me. Some of the pressure I put on you then wasn't just about whether James could be mine but must have been tied up with my increasingly bad feelings about Nicola. I was pretty mixed up."

At last he looked into his wife's eyes, and his rueful smile gave her hope. He hadn't quite apologised, but maybe things weren't as bad as she had feared.

"In the end," he went on, "I was really desperate to put the affair behind me and be just with you and the family; I knew that was what I really wanted. I ended it the kindest way I could think of: I got her promoted to head office in London, with a decent salary raise. She made a bit of a meal about accepting it – my heart was in my mouth for a few days – but she did, and we had a tearful farewell – well, she was tearful, I just tried to be nice – four or five months before James was born. She sent me one or two rather strange letters after that, but I didn't answer them, and I haven't heard from her since. And I left Capital, changed jobs. End of story."

Kate moved over to him, knelt on the floor beside his chair, and chose her words with care.

"I get the feeling we are going to survive this." She put her hand on his. "But there is one more twist to this whole sad saga, and I fear it will come as a shock, but it may help you see things my way. A few years ago, at another of these blessed Christmas parties, Andrew, your old colleague from Capital, told me that he had seen Nicola at a head office family picnic, talked to her and her husband, learnt they had a child, almost the same age as James."

Trevor looked stunned. He stood up and turned to her, lifted her to her feet and took her into his arms.

They stood motionless for what seemed an age. Taking the initiative again, she led him to the sofa. They sat down side by side, still silent, but close. She rested her head on his shoulder and held his hand.

"That was hard."

He squeezed her hand and, almost for the first time that afternoon, looked at her properly. Her face showed the deep sorrow, the strain – and yet the love – and he was deeply moved.

"You know, you're beautiful even when you're unhappy." He paused before continuing, his voice breaking a little. "I'm sorry. I'm very, very sorry. I can see things a bit differently now, though if I'm honest, I'll still have to adjust to the Jonathan and James affair. I guess it's a man thing, this gut reaction... I feel... I don't know... I can't explain. I know I was wrong, stupidly wrong to have the affair with Nicola, and I can't believe you knew and said nothing. But my anger at you about James, I just couldn't hide it any longer... but how I could be so cruel as to tell you I knew about him like that..."

He shook his head in disbelief and looked down at her. "Can we really get over this?"

In answer, she raised her head from his shoulder and gave him the lightest of kisses on the mouth. "We are certainly going to try, and I think – I am pretty sure – we will. I care desperately about us as a family. And when I said just now that I still love you, I meant it."

"It doesn't seem quite right just to reply 'I love you too'." Trevor's voice trembled a little. "It's too easily said – you might find it hard to believe after these recent months – but I… I believe I do, deeply. And it's not all I feel: I can't tell you how grateful I am, how much I admire you – and how sorry I am." He turned a little and took her face in his hands. "You mean everything to me," he almost whispered. He returned her kiss as lightly as before and began stroking her thighs, reaching the suspender clip under her skirt.

"Did you put these on specially for me?" Visibly emotionally wracked as he was, an inadvertent twinkle came into his eyes as he realised she had noticed him hardening. He looked at her apologetically. "Sorry. This is probably the last thing you want from me right now."

She didn't answer immediately but pulled him closer to her.

"No, you're wrong. I think this is just the right way to start afresh." And she began to undo his shirt but stopped before getting very far. "Just a minute. Stand up a moment, please."

Trevor obeyed, puzzled, but she explained as she slowly undressed him:

"I want to see the underneath you, the undecorated, naked you; the man I have slept beside and with for so long. I want to rediscover you." She stood back to admire him.

"I can see what Nicola was after," she said with a grin. "Not bad at all for forty! And those little silver streaks – gorgeous." She reached up to touch the silver at his temples, svelte contrast to his still thick, dark hair, then stroked his chest with its light scattering of black hair and ran her hands down lower and lower until she was aware that he was almost trembling with desire.

"May I have the same privilege?" he asked with a smile, forcing himself to hold back.

Kate loosened her belt and let him drop her skirt and lift her sweater over her head until she stood there in the lacy underwear she had chosen so carefully that morning. His eyes widened involuntarily as she slowly unfastened the stockings and rolled them down. He unhooked her lacy white bra, slipped off the matching panties and the suspender belt with its little blue bows above the clips, and folded her to him. The stresses of the afternoon melted away as they held one another tight, skin to skin, and rediscovered the pleasures, the smell, taste and feel of each other.

They sank to the floor and made first leisurely, then increasingly urgent love. Sated, they lay spread-eagled on the soft carpet, holding hands, breathless, until Kate caught sight of the mantelpiece clock.

"Heavens above, it's almost five; nearly time to get the boys from Ann's!" She freed her hand. "Race you to the shower!"

Laughing, and acting half his age, Trevor followed her upstairs and into the over-size shower they had installed in their bathroom in a fit of extravagance when they bought the house. There they soaped each other all over and stood close under the steaming jet before pulling apart and emerging into normality.

"Shall we both go for the boys?" Trevor grunted as he pulled on fresh clothes.

"No, you go, and I'll tidy up – lunch is still on the table, and our clothes are all over the sitting room floor." She didn't want to have to go into explanations to the boys about what they had been up to, why the house was so untidy. "The boys won't be hungry after the barbecue. I'll think about what we could eat – would you mind a take-away?" She had put a lot of thought into the pre-showdown lunch but hadn't got as far as the evening.

"No, that's fine. You choose. I'll see you in about half an hour – and I shall thank Ann particularly warmly for having them for so long!" He gave her a sideways glance.

Kate waved from the doorstep as he went to his car, then turned back into the house, glad to be alone for a moment. She sat down on the so-recently vacated sofa and looked at the mess of their clothes on the floor. It had worked, but in spite of a heady mixture of triumph and relief, she felt drained, and not as confident about the future as she had let him think. Although she was sure he would stay, that they had a future together, she wondered how long it would be before they would be totally relaxed with each other. How much talking should they do? How much going over the ground? Sex alone would not heal the wounds. We may even find ourselves back at the counsellor's, she thought briefly, before dismissing the idea with a shudder.

Deciding that this was not the moment for deep thought, she tidied the room, put the crumpled clothes into the laundry room, and set to work in the kitchen. She knew she ran an excellent home and had made herself a pillar of support to Trevor and did not resent it. She enjoyed her weekly volunteering at the Millcrest Foundation's charity shop and also edited their supporter newsletter, believing strongly in the work they did helping youngsters reach their full potential. But now that all the boys were at school, so much more was possible. Looking forward to the challenge of something different, she had already downloaded the Open University prospectus onto her laptop to see if any degree courses appealed.

She found the number of their favourite Chinese restaurant, ordered, and checked that all was straight again before sitting down in the kitchen with the untouched morning paper to await the return of her menfolk.

Chapter 6

Trevor drove carefully out into the traffic. He too felt a mix of emotions; sexual euphoria was still uppermost, but he found himself strangely reluctant to explore the underlying churning of his mind. To help keep his thoughts under control, he turned on the radio to catch the news, but soon found he couldn't concentrate. It was not far to Ann's house and as he turned into her street, it suddenly hit him that he was to be faced with the child he now knew for certain was not his – and not just that: he was now so very aware of the circumstances in which James had been conceived.

Suddenly overcome with the enormity of the afternoon's revelations, he pulled in to the side of the road and turned the engine off. He found that he was trembling; the healing of that torrid but so intimate interlude was far from complete, he realised. He folded his arms over the steering wheel and let his head sink onto them, willed himself to relax. James, and the other two, must not detect any difference in him, he knew. But how difficult to be completely natural; how hard not to cast covert glances at James and torture himself again with his likeness to Jonathan Markham.

Taking a deep breath, he started the engine and drove on, parked in Ann's drive and rang the bell. Charlie and Paul were first to the door, with little James pushing forward under their arms, all eager to tell him about their day. Ann appeared behind them, smiling and, to Trevor's relief, showing no sign of awareness of why she had been enlisted as an accomplice.

"That was really kind of you, Ann. I can see from their faces they've had a lovely time. What do you say, boys?"

"Thank you, Ann. It was a super afternoon. Can Mike and Peter come to us soon?" Charlie spoke first, the other two nodded enthusiastically in agreement.

Mike and Peter looked hopefully at their mother.

"I know they'd love to," Ann smiled as she and her boys waved them off.

The journey home was easier than he had expected. The boys, filling the back seat of the car with restless energy, chattered at him the whole way home. Overexcited from the day's activities, each clamouring to be heard, they left him no space to worry about his demeanour.

Once home and handed over to Kate for a bath, the boys had calmed down by the time he took up his usual role of bedtime story reader, the time he loved best of all and which he really missed when he was away from home. With all three snuggled up beside him on James's bed, he felt a rush of love for them and happily entertained them with the exploits of Pooh and Piglet. He found he had no qualms tucking an exhausted James into bed before moving on to the older boys' room for a chapter of Harry Potter. Then they too were tucked in, and Kate was called up for their goodnight kiss.

Trevor went downstairs and opened a bottle of white wine from the fridge, took glasses and savoury biscuits into the sitting room and poured the wine ready for her reappearance. Once again, the events of the afternoon raced through his mind, and the doubt about how natural they could be with one another resurfaced. He had no time to plan his approach, however, before Kate came in looking surprisingly unruffled. He wondered whether, underneath, she was as nervous as he was.

She laid her hand briefly on his shoulder and picked up her glass. She stood in front of him and held it up: "Here's to us and our future together." He raised his glass in answer, and their eyes locked in mutual awareness of the difficulties which they had independently realised lay ahead.

She sat down, not beside him but opposite, and took a sip of wine.

"I've ordered Chinese and it should be here in twenty minutes or so. The table's laid in the kitchen." She paused for a moment, then continued: "Look, I know we're going to feel a bit strange with one another for a while, but this evening let's just pretend everything is normal – let's practise, if you like – and not go over it all. OK?"

Trevor nodded gratefully, blessing her for her tact and happy to delay any post mortems or recriminations, though he had an uncomfortable feeling that they would not be avoidable for ever. They drank their wine companionably enough, talking about the boys and their exciting day, until the doorbell rang.

"You get it and pay; I'll put the kettle on." Kate disappeared into the kitchen, while he took the delivery. Then, the food unpacked and a pot of jasmine tea made, they sat and began eating. Trevor was pleased Kate had chosen the crispy duck. The sharing out of the components, the ritual rolling up of the filled pancakes, and the messiness of eating them were oddly intimate. They ate slowly, perhaps unconsciously postponing the next stage of the evening.

The meal could be drawn out no longer; the table was cleared, the dishwasher loaded.

"Coffee?" Trevor moved towards the kettle.

"No thanks, not after all that wine and tea. Do you mind if I have an early bath and go to bed now? I'm exhausted." Kate looked at him hesitantly. "And I don't know how you feel, but I'm not sure I'm up for more sex, so perhaps we could just snuggle up together tonight."

Trevor felt a quick stab of desire but found he was also rather relieved at her suggestion. But even as he concurred, he wondered whether this was right. Would it not seem even more difficult tomorrow?

He allowed Kate a luxurious length of bath time before joining her. She was in bed but not pretending to be asleep, he was glad to see. His ablutions quickly completed, he slid in beside her and turned off his bedside light. She moved towards him and laid her head in the familiar hollow formed by his neck and shoulder. The silky fabric of her nightdress slid against his bare chest and he had to concentrate hard to remain unaroused.

"I'm so glad we survived today," she said. "I wouldn't want to go through that again for anything. To think how close we came to destroying everything – but let's not talk about it any more tonight." She ran a finger across his lips, then raised her head enough to give him a quick kiss. Lowering herself down again, she slid her arms around him and held him close for a few seconds before moving away, whispering, "Good night, my love. Sleep well."

Trevor planted a light kiss on her back and turned away, wondering how long it would take his still-racing mind to calm enough for sleep.

Chapter 7

Sleep came more quickly than Trevor had expected, and he woke to find the sun creeping in through the slight gap in the curtains, casting flickering shadows on the bed as the trees outside the window waved in what promised to be a strong wind. Kate was still asleep as he crept out of bed, and he paused a moment to take in the familiar face, slightly crumpled from sleep, but relaxed and peaceful. Emerging onto the landing, he heard voices coming from Charlie and Paul's room at the end of the hall, and he found all three boys intent on setting up the toy fort, a present to Paul from Kate's parents for his recent eighth birthday.

Squatting down on the floor with them, he became totally absorbed in their endeavours. Paul masterminded the operation, reading only slightly hesitantly from the instructions, and Charlie exercised unusual self-restraint in not grabbing them from his younger brother and taking control. James busied himself lining up toy soldiers and dinosaurs indiscriminately, ready to occupy the fort, quite unconcerned at the incongruity. He was charming in his concentration, broken only by Trevor's occasional questions.

"What's this one with the spiny back?" Trevor pointed.

"Tyrannosaurus Rex. It's very nasty."

"And this one?"

"Diplodocus. It's huge, it can knock all the invaders down."

What was it with little boys and dinosaurs, Trevor wondered? Why the fascination? Is my other son the same?

That last thought brought him up short, the reality of this unknown child. Was it in fact a boy? He tried hard to think back to the day before. What exactly had Kate said? Nicola had introduced the colleague to her husband and her child. *He* was the same age as James? *She* was the same age as James? He was pretty sure it was 'he', but how could he be certain? He tried imagining asking Kate if it was a boy or a girl but flinched from the idea.

Maybe it didn't matter. After all, this child would not be part of his life; he hadn't even known about it the day before so it couldn't – shouldn't – be important. He closed his mind to the question and returned his attention to the boys. The fort was almost complete.

"Well done, boys. That's brilliant." He picked up a toy drum from the shelf and rat-tatted a fanfare as James marched the soldiers and dinosaurs up to the drawbridge. The noise was so great they didn't hear the door open and Kate come in. She stood behind them watching, a smile lighting her face.

After a few moments she broke the spell, clapping in time to the drum.

"Well done you three, that's fantastic. You'll have loads of fun with it, but now it's time for breakfast."

A little more encouragement was needed to drag them away as they continued to play.

"This will bite you if you don't come down NOW!" Trevor chased them through the door with a dinosaur.

The chaos of family breakfast, the arguments over Weetabix and Frosties, the demands for toast, coffee, juice, more butter please, increased the feel of family normality, and both Kate and Trevor relaxed.

Breakfast over, the boys dragged Trevor back upstairs to play with the fort. Kate sat down with the Sunday papers, prepared lunch, called them down – all so very normal.

After lunch came clamours for a family expedition:

"Please, please, can we go to the Downs and take the kites?"

"It's so windy."

"We haven't flown them for ages."

Laughing, Trevor went to fetch the kites from the garage while Kate equipped everyone with coats.

It was only a short drive to the wide open spaces of the Downs. It was true, the wind was quite fierce, and the boys and Trevor struggled to get all three kites airborne and under control. Charlie, with a ten-year-old's ambition, wanted to try loops but the wind was too strong and he soon gave up and joined Paul in competing to get their kite the highest. James was just thrilled to keep his kite safely in the air. Trevor and Kate stood side by side watching the boys' fierce concentration.

As they stood there, Trevor was suddenly very aware of the closeness of Kate's body. Moving slightly so that their shoulders were touching, he slipped his arm around her waist and pulled her into him. He leant down a little.

"Thank you," he murmured in her ear. "Thank you for standing by me, for stopping me from ruining everything. I know how lucky I am."

Kate looked up at him with a slight smile, though her eyes were still sad. He found himself moved again by her generosity, and a surge of love passed through him. He turned her face towards him with his free hand and kissed her lightly on the lips, then, overcome, let his emotions flow in a deep kiss which took them both by surprise.

It was some moments before titters and snorts told them the boys were watching, simultaneously amused and embarrassed. They broke apart grinning and turned their attention once more to the kites. It was tiring in the strong wind, and the boys had soon had enough.

Back at the house, tea refreshed and re-energised everyone. There was time for play before the daily allowance of television before supper and bed.

"Are there any leftovers in the fridge? Can I rustle up something for supper?" Trevor didn't often cook but enjoyed exercising a bit of imagination from time to time; his mother had always said that being able to make up a decent meal from whatever there was in the cupboard was the sign of a good cook. "You read to the boys for a change."

Kate accepted gratefully; she too liked cooking, but the repetitious nature of cooking for a family every day took the fun out of it. By the time she came downstairs again, there were tempting smells of garlic and sausage, and she sniffed the air appreciatively as she entered the kitchen. The table was laid, a bowl of salad, an open bottle of wine and candles graced the centre, and Trevor was draining pasta into the sink.

"Perfect timing, darling. Light the candles, pour the wine, and sit down and relax." He turned back to the stove and mixed the contents of a frying pan into the pasta, sprinkled chopped basil on top, and finished it all off with Parmesan shavings. "Voila! Dinner is served!" He put the dish down with a flourish. "Just the leftovers from yesterday's lunch, and a few bits and pieces."

Kate served them both. "This is delicious!" she exclaimed. "I don't know how you do it!"

Trevor grinned. "I was inspired by you this evening." He reached across and touched her hand. The electricity flowed again as she raised her glass to him and looked him in the eye and they both knew that bed would be early and energetic that night.

Energetic it was, and loving too, and afterwards they held each other close for a few moments before turning away from each other to sleep.

"Good night," murmured Kate. "Sleep well – work tomorrow."

Trevor felt for her hand and squeezed it gently before curling up in his habitual pose.

However, he was surprised that sleep didn't come as quickly as the night before, in spite of the good feelings he now had about his marriage and his and Kate's ability to be comfortable together again. Restless, he tried his usual sleep-inducing tricks: trying to work out how many airports he had visited; how many rivers he could think of beginning with successive letters of the alphabet. But he found his mind going back over the day, focusing mostly on the boys and how relieved he was that their family would remain intact.

But then the thought of his other son – child – intruded again and he began to speculate about whether it looked like him or like Nicola. And about how her husband felt about having a stepson – child – and whether the child had been told he wasn't the real father. He wondered how old the child had been when Nicola married, guessing at least one or two. He was disconcerted to realise how badly he wanted to know if it was a boy or a girl. How could he possibly find out? He knew he couldn't ask Kate; it would be too painful.

He finally fell asleep, only to be woken all too soon by the alarm and the necessity of stepping straight into the work and school day routine. Kate was already in the shower as he forced himself out of bed. She gave him a damp peck on the cheek as he stood shaving and went to rouse the boys before getting dressed herself.

Although the school was within walking distance, at least for the older two, they were still too young to walk alone and Kate took them by car, sharing the home run with Ann. Trevor always drove to work, an easy twenty minutes unless Bristol's traffic was even worse than usual.

This morning he set off with a light heart, and though still yawning, felt ready to tackle the day. He enjoyed his job with Staffords, the big commercial property company he had moved to four years before. It had several major offices in the UK and overseas, as well as prestigious headquarters in Hanover Square. Managing the Bristol office was a sufficient challenge to satisfy Trevor's considerable ambition, at least for another year or two. He didn't envy head office people the dirt, noise and crowds of London, or its frenetic pace, he thought as he negotiated the still-quiet city centre. "I wonder how Nicola liked it?" The thought popped into his head unbidden and was quickly followed by: "It's not a great place to bring up small children."

"Damn," he said to himself as he drove into the company garage. "Damn. I must stop thinking about it." He forced himself to clear his mind and focus on the day ahead as he locked the car and went up in the lift to his office.

Chapter 8

"Good morning, Trevor. Had a good weekend?" Virginia, his secretary, looked up from her desk and smiled.

"Yes, thanks," Trevor replied, putting the trauma of the past few days into a mental file and locking it, ready for a busy office week. "You too, I hope. You're in early."

"Yes, plenty to do, and I wanted to beat the traffic. There's an important email for you from head office; they want you in London next week, Wednesday and Thursday. Seems there's a big deal coming up. I've checked your diary, looks OK."

Trevor nodded non-committally, went straight through to his office, fired up his computer and found the relevant email. There wasn't much background, just that a meeting was being called to discuss a possible major deal which would be managed by the Bristol office if it went through. There was plenty of work to keep him occupied, and his thoughts rarely strayed to London and his child.

That evening, over supper when the children were in bed, he broached the subject.

"Had an email from head office today. They want me in London Wednesday and Thursday next week, seems there's a big deal coming up. No details yet. Is that OK? Nothing in the diary I'll have to back out of?"

"No, that's fine. I can take the boys to swimming Wednesday evening, no problem."

To Trevor's relief, Kate seemed relaxed about his forthcoming days in London. She clearly didn't notice his occasional abstraction, and he fought to keep it that way. They found it increasingly easy to behave as if nothing had happened, though he was sure that she, as he, had it at the back of her mind. Would they ever really forget, he wondered, even if life became as untroubled as before? Would they ever regain their mutual trust?

Wednesday came, and Trevor took an early train to London, his overnight bag packed by Kate as usual – she had handed it to him with a wry smile but no comment on the previous time she had packed for him, when he had left so abruptly after their disastrous visit to the counsellor. His heart sank as he realised he would not have the distraction of Kate and the boys to keep his mind in check outside working hours.

He spent the journey reading the papers he had received for the meeting, and was at head office in time to greet colleagues who had flown in from Germany and France to discuss the possible big development opportunity. He was disconcerted to find one was Horst, an erstwhile colleague from Capital Property, the company he had worked for during the Nicola episode. And to his embarrassment, after expressions of mutual pleasure at both having moved to Staffords, Horst opened the conversation with an enquiry after her.

"How is she, that girl? Quite a looker, she was, and not too many scruples, I thought. She obviously fancied you something rotten. Did she make a move on you?"

Trevor cursed Horst's powers of observation and his fluency in English idioms. He agreed half-heartedly about her looks, and avoided answering the direct question, though he could see Horst looking at him speculatively.

"She was promoted to Capital's UK head office not too long after that German trip when you met her. I haven't been in touch or heard of her since, so I don't know if she's still with them." That last statement at least was true.

Fortunately, they were interrupted by more colleagues coming in. Trevor introduced Horst and they all moved to the conference room for the briefing. The project was complicated, a possible major light industrial and retail complex outside Bristol, and required total concentration. The time passed quickly until lunch.

"Excuse me a moment, gentlemen. I'll be with you shortly." Trevor indicated the stairs up to the company dining room, turned the other way and found an empty office. He sat looking at the telephone, wrestling with his conscience and his increasingly overwhelming desire to find out more about his child. After a few minutes of inaction, he stood up and marched himself out to join his colleagues, sadly aware that this was but the first of such battles he would be fighting.

It was only about 4.30 when the afternoon meeting finished, and dinner had been arranged for 7.30. Trevor left the office and went to his nearby hotel, intending to sleep for an hour or so and then shower before going out again. He flung his overnight bag and suit jacket onto the armchair, sat down on the bed and pulled his shoes off. He lay back against the pillows and closed his eyes. But that niggling desire was still there. Sitting up, he took out his iPhone, but innate caution prevailed and he picked up the hotel phone. The hotel operator answered immediately.

"Please can you put me through to Capital Property." His heart was pounding and his mouth was dry. I shan't be speaking to her, he told himself, but he didn't know what he was going to say when the call came.

When the phone rang, it made him jump. He answered it immediately.

"You're through, sir," said the operator, and he heard another woman's voice: "Capital Property. How can I help you?"

"I am looking for an old colleague who worked for Capital. Nicola Johnson, she was a legal assistant, about five or six years ago. Does she still work for the company?"

"I don't know, sir, I'll put you through to the legal section. Hold the line, please."

Trevor almost hung up at this point. Suppose Nicola herself came on the line. What on earth would he say? He thought perhaps he would just hang up rather than explain himself. He didn't try to think through what he was actually hoping to achieve by this call.

To his utmost relief, a man's voice came on the line: "Legal department, Brian Jenkins speaking. Can I help you?"

"My name is..." In a flash, Trevor realised he didn't want to give his name in case he was put through to Nicola, or that she heard about his call. "My name is Alan Rose," getting inspiration from the flowery pictures on the wall opposite the bed. "I used to work with Nicola Johnson. Is she still with Capital?"

"No, she left about five years ago. Is this a personal call?"

"Yes, I'm an old friend and colleague. I'm in town for a couple of days and thought to look her up and chat over old times." Trevor held his breath. One half of him didn't want to know, but the other half had its metaphorical fingers crossed.

"Sorry," said the disembodied Brian. "She married a colleague, Michael Bryant, and left to have a baby. I think she came back to the company part time for a while. I heard they moved to Wimbledon, but I don't know any details."

Trevor's heart sank more than he felt it should. Relief at Nicola not being in the company had been replaced by disappointment.

"OK, thanks anyway," he said, and hung up.

He lay there on the bed, forcing himself to relax, and slowly sleep took over. He woke with only the minimum time to shower and change before dinner with his colleagues.

******

The next day's meetings were as intense as the first, and it became clear that this was a seriously big project which would require his presence in London for meetings for several weeks, if not months. If it went ahead it would be a coup for the Bristol office and an interesting and demanding personal challenge for him: negotiations with local and central government, maybe the EU too, and building relationships with the critical and environmentally aware Bristol citizens.

Trevor was able to get away to catch the train which would get him home in time to read to the children before bed, and as he always did, he called Kate to say he was on his way. At Paddington, with a bit of time to spare, he wandered into the newsagent thinking to pick up something to read other than the evening paper. Next to the papers was a shelf of London guides, with a prominent display of A-Zs. On impulse, he picked one up and flicked through. Wimbledon. There it was, not far south of the river. Judging from the size of the green area labelled 'Wimbledon Common', it was quite a leafy district, close to Richmond Park, too. Returning the book to the shelf, he collected an evening paper from the pile outside the shop for the journey back to Bristol.

The boys were thrilled to have him home in time for their bedtime stories. James demanded more of Pooh and was hard to settle as he imitated first Pooh eating honey, and then the heffalump trudging round the bedroom. Once James was in bed with the light off, Trevor went across the hall to Charlie and Paul. They were enthusiastic listeners to Harry Potter, but their pleas for "one more chapter, one more chapter, please!" fell on deaf ears as Kate called Trevor down to supper. He hugged them both and deposited kisses on their heads.

"You can read quietly for ten minutes, but then lights out. I don't want to have to come up and put them out for you," he admonished, and went down to supper.

He sat at the kitchen table, watching as Kate put the finishing touches to the meal then served them both. As they ate, he told her about the meetings and the importance of this project, confessing that he would have to go to London fairly regularly for a few weeks. She nodded, apparently unconcerned, but Trevor couldn't help wondering what was going through her mind. He told her about the coincidence of Horst having moved to Staffords, but not about his views on Nicola. That seemed wise, rather than deception.

Chapter 9

Routine reasserted itself, helping their relationship to return almost to normal more quickly than they had dared to hope. Their love-making was frequent, and more passionate than it had been for months.

One Saturday afternoon when the boys were all out with friends, Trevor cast a sideways look at Kate, raised a questioning eyebrow, and nodded his head in the direction of the stairs. Kate pretended not to understand until he said, "Feel like some horizontal exercise, Mrs Martin?"

The next time they found themselves at home alone, Kate was more direct, sliding behind him, running her hand down his chest and kissing the back of his neck. "I fancy you something rotten, right now," she whispered into his hair and led him to that very same carpet on which their first healing intercourse had taken place.

******

Day to day, to his relief, Trevor found that most of the time he was able to control his wandering mind. He took huge pleasure in the boys and almost never thought of James as anything but his own son. He didn't need Kate to remind him that James should never suspect he had been the cause of that terrible time.

However, his speculations about his other child grew more frequent as the next London meeting approached. One day, in a quiet moment at the office, persuading himself it was pure curiosity, he checked on Google Maps and found that Wimbledon's postal district was SW19. Almost holding his breath, as a way to get started he went to the directory enquiries site on the web and searched for Bryant, Michael in SW19. He was very aware of his thumping heart as he found a Michael Bryant, and two M. Bryants. He told himself that 'his' Michael Bryant might have an unlisted number, and anyway, it was only an idle enquiry. However, he noted down the addresses and numbers provided on the site in his electronic diary 'just in case', sure Kate didn't know his password. As he did so, he suspected his guilt was visible in his face. He certainly felt uncomfortable.

Trevor took his usual early train to the London meeting, also a two-day one. But this time, instead of putting his mind entirely to the business ahead, he spent some time in a reverie, imagining Wimbledon, thinking about what it might be like for a young child living there. By the time the train pulled into Paddington, a plan was half formed in his head, though he admitted to himself that he was ashamed to be allowing such ideas to take hold.

Horst was not at the meeting, Trevor was glad to see, and there was less pressure to be sociable in the evening.

"I hope you don't mind if I don't join you for dinner," he said as his colleagues packed up their papers at the end of the afternoon. "It's been a long day and I've some Bristol work to get through. I'll see you tomorrow, 9.30." Avoiding their eyes, he raised his hand in farewell as he left the room.

But rather than going to his hotel, he joined the rush hour throng making its way to Green Park tube station.

The journey to Wimbledon was easy, just a change at Earls Court, but uncomfortably crowded. Balancing himself against a partition, he spent the time looking up the three Bryant addresses on his phone and planning the walk between them. Two were reasonably close to each other, the third some distance but still walkable, and he had plenty of time. He was not sure what he would do when he found these addresses, except that he hoped to be able to find where Nicola lived. Further, he hadn't allowed himself to think.

Arrived at Wimbledon station, he set out on his planned route. It was a chilly evening, so he stepped out strongly, away from the shopping area into the grid of residential streets. The first address, one of the M. Bryants, was a block of flats, clearly privately owned, but nonetheless rather mean and forbidding. Not logically, perhaps, but optimistically, he decided this couldn't be where Nicola and their son would live. He had decided it had to be a boy; after all, fathers determined the sex of a child, and he had three – no two, he hurriedly corrected himself – sons already.

He walked on to the next address, the Michael Bryant in full. This was much more promising: a smallish but attractive Edwardian semi in a street of well-tended houses, some with cars squeezed into the little front gardens. This Michael Bryant's house had no car space but the garden was bright with Michaelmas daisies and chrysanthemums round a tidy lawn. He stood at a discreet distance for a moment, looking for clues as to the occupants, but there was no evidence to help determine what sort of people, young or older, lived there. He moved on.

His final destination was the other side of the High Street, towards the All England Tennis Club. It was getting dark by then and he had to pause under street lights from time to time to check his route. The roads became wider and leafier, the houses bigger, the cars in driveways distinctly more expensive. As he neared his destination, he began to feel more self-conscious, more intrusive; somehow these houses had a keep-away feel to them.

The street was wide, with grass verges planted with mature trees, some beginning to show their autumn colours. The house was red brick, probably built between the wars, and as big as his own in Bristol, but clearly worth a great deal more money in this neighbourhood. A double garage at the side had a small, silver Mercedes saloon parked in front of it. The gates to the paved driveway beside the trim lawn of the big front garden were open, but there was no sign of life apart from a light in the hall and another in a window at the side.

Trevor stood on the pavement outside, his emotions mixed. Had Nicola really done so well for herself? Would the boy be at some posh pre-prep school, destined for a major public school? He felt slightly uncomfortable at that. The boys at home were all at state schools. His own parents had had very little money and considered themselves working class, so he had attended the nearest primary school and then a state comprehensive. He had been lucky with the latter. He remembered his mother's pride when she had reported back to him after one parents' evening. "The teachers were very nice about you," Mrs Martin had said, beaming. "They say you must take A levels and go to university. My, that would be quite something for our family."

He had not felt comfortable with the idea of private schooling for his boys, even though that had been Kate's preference, based on her own education, and she had argued quite hard for it. Indeed, it had been their first serious disagreement. But finally, having interviewed the local state primary, she had fallen in with his wishes.

"OK, if you feel that strongly," she had said. "And you're right that they're more likely to make local friends. But, please, promise me you'll reconsider if we don't feel they're getting what they need." Trevor had duly promised.

As he continued to stand there watching the house, Trevor reflected how far he had come since his own childhood. His father had been intelligent and very well read for a man of his background but had lacked ambition and followed his own father into the building trade. For some years he worked for a big company in London which was engaged in demolition and related work. The dust had affected his lungs and doctors told him he should move away from the polluted atmosphere of

London and his building trade. So when Trevor was seven, the family moved from their council house in Southwark to the outskirts of Bristol, where a cousin who lived in that area had said he might be able to help in finding work.

Later, having built a reputation as a good and reliable general handyman, his father managed to buy a dilapidated cottage in the countryside south of Bristol which he painstakingly renovated over the years. He embraced gardening with enthusiasm, growing fruit and vegetables as well as flowers, and entering all the local horticultural competitions. He was very proud of his success.

"Look, Susan," Trevor remembered his father saying as he held a giant cabbage in one hand and a gold-starred certificate in the other. With remarkable sleight of hand, the cabbage and certificate were replaced with an enormous turnip and another gold star. "Two firsts, and a 'highly commended' for my carrots, too, and another one for that pink geranium I've kept going these past three years."

"Well done, love, they'll make good eating – do several dinners!" His mother had patted her husband on the back and given him a quick peck on the cheek. "Come and have your tea."

His mother had taken work as a cleaner to supplement the family income. Having seen how more affluent people lived, plus the teachers' encouragement, Trevor knew that she had begun to envisage a better future for him, their only child. She'd given him glimpses into another world, occasionally taking him with her to meet her employers and see their houses. His teachers' and mother's belief in him had proved justified, and his A-level grades were high enough to give him a wide choice of good universities. He had chosen Bristol so he could live cheaply at home.

Trevor had confessed to Kate when they were both back at university after the long summer break, Kate for her final year, that he had chosen the MA rather than going straight into a traineeship so that he could be with her. He admitted that it was his modest background which had made him shy of accepting Kate's invitation to meet her parents, and that it had been with trepidation that he had finally introduced her to his.

Kate, however, had been marvellous: strengthening his love and admiration for her by choosing only to see how hard his parents had worked, achieving not only a successful small business and a cosy if modest home, but also being so supportive of their only child and encouraging him to develop his potential.

He remembered all too well his first foray into Old Rectory country. He had been horribly nervous, but he had seen enough with his mother's help to understand how such people lived, and so to cope with their hospitality. He guessed Kate had prepared her parents well; they had hidden any doubts they may have had about him as a possible son-in-law and welcomed him kindly. Trevor's father's gardening passion proved a useful talking point with Mrs Adamson, and over the weekend Mr Adamson, obviously impressed with Trevor's intelligence and industry, opened a conversation about his future.

"I've enjoyed talking with you, Trevor. You've a good, sharp mind, and I think you could go places. If you like, when the time comes, I could give you some introductions to legal firms I've had dealings with in the City."

"That's very kind of you Mr Adamson, and hugely appreciated." He swallowed, then went on: "I don't know what Kate has said to you, but I'm sure you've gathered that..." He paused, fumbling for a suitable phrase. "That I'm very fond of her. I wouldn't be here, I guess, if she didn't feel something for me." Trevor hesitated again before continuing shyly. "I hope maybe, when the time is right, I might ask her to marry me – I mean, I might ask you for your permission to ask her," suddenly remembering the protocol from the period novels in the English GCSE syllabus. "I really want to be a good husband and provide well for Kate. It's a great incentive to make something of my career."

Mr Adamson smiled and nodded. "I had a feeling that might be in the air. I look forward to a future conversation." He held out his hand for Trevor to shake, as if sealing a contract.

The dogs took to him, too, demanding stick or ball throwing, and bestowing many slobbery licks. On a walk with them to the local woods, Trevor confessed his conversation with her father to Kate. She took his hands in hers. "That was brave of you. I hope you won't wait too long for that permission!" The dogs were ignored for the duration of a long kiss.

On top of his desire to be worthy of Kate and show he could fit in with her circle, her father's faith in him had been an additional spur and he had worked hard to achieve his success as a commercial property lawyer. He could look at this big Wimbledon house and know he, too, had done well.

Trevor was still lost in thought when he heard the front door closing. His stomach turned over and he dived for the shadow cast by a large oak tree. His heart and breath returned to normal as he saw an older woman, slim and smartly dressed – definitely not Nicola – who went straight to the car, opened the door and got in. Trevor moved behind the tree and watched as she backed out into the road, glancing at him before driving off.

Who was she? Was this Nicola's house and this her mother or mother-in-law? Or was this the woman's house? Or was she just a visitor? There was no way of knowing, and Trevor emerged from the shadows feeling rather stupid, and ashamed of his furtive behaviour. He really must take a grip on himself, he thought, as he retraced his steps to the tube station.

Back at his hotel, Trevor, hungry after his extended walk, took himself down to the main restaurant for a late dinner. Eating alone gave him time to think and castigate himself. What, honestly, did he hope to achieve by this detective work? What would Kate think if she found out? The very idea made his blood run cold. Draining the last of the second glass of wine he had allowed himself with his steak, he promised her silently that he would do no more of it.

The next day he was again able to get home in good time. Kate met him in the hall as he opened the door. He gave her a big hug, and told her, speaking from the heart, how glad he was to be home. Kate smiled up at him.

"Sit down and relax with a drink for half an hour while I get the boys ready for bed," she said, giving him a quick kiss. "Then I'll put supper on the table while you read to them."

Later, passing her on the stairs on his way to the bedtime reading session, he put out a hand to stop her descent and kissed her on the lips.

"I love you."

Kate looked surprised at the moment he had chosen, but the look in his eyes told her he meant it. She gave his hand a squeeze.

"Let's have a bottle of wine with supper," she said. "It's only a light meal as I know you're tired, but let's make it a bit special." She disappeared down into the kitchen.

His resolution of the night before made him feel strong and protective of her, and it was an intimate and contented meal, which only made him more determined to put the speculation behind him. Later, in bed, he held her close and again told her he loved her. Their love-making was gentle and satisfying. He slept well.

Chapter 10

Work continued to keep Trevor busy in Bristol. His stints in London ceased as the big deal had been put on hold for a few months, and he was increasingly able to put his secret investigations behind him and was pleased with his self-control. Licked it! he thought to himself more than once.

However, as Christmas neared, Trevor and Kate took the boys to the golf club's children's party. There was quite a crowd present, including Jonathan Markham and his family. Trevor was helping with a game when he turned round to see Kate holding James's hand and talking to Jonathan who was looking appraisingly – admiringly – at James, clearly the subject of their conversation. The likeness between father and son, the shape of their noses, their long jaws, and their reddish-blond hair, was quite noticeable, at least to Trevor's unhappy eye. He wondered whether any of the other people could see it. Jealousy and anger leapt to the surface, and he clenched his fists and turned away to avoid showing his feelings.

Trevor forced himself to relax but kept his distance until the game finished. Then, going over to Kate who had released James for his next game, he asked pointedly after Jonathan. Kate glanced sideways at him, clearly aware of his mood. She started to reach to take his hand but withdrew with a barely audible sigh and turned her attention back to the boys who were lining up for tea.

The party drew to a close; it only remained for the children to file past Father Christmas to collect their going home presents. Kate and Trevor gathered the excited boys and their goody bags and returned to the car. The drive home, while not silent as the children chattered away, was not companionable.

That evening, over coffee in the sitting room after supper, Kate raised the subject.

"I saw your reaction when I was talking to Jonathan at the party. Please, darling, don't start down that jealousy route again." She moved to his chair and knelt down in front of him, took his hands in hers and looked up into his eyes. "I told you before, and I swear to you again, that there is nothing, nothing at all, between Jonathan and me. James is a beautiful, intelligent child, anyone would admire him, but how he is as a person is down to us. We – you and I – are his parents, no-one else. I can't ignore Jonathan at these social events, it would be just too pointed. People, especially his wife, would think there really was, or had been, something between us."

"I know, I know. I thought I was getting over this, but it seems not. It's hard." Trevor was on the point of saying how he would love the chance to be able to see how his own son – he was still sure it had to be a boy – looked, but bit it back, unsure if it was wise to raise the Nicola subject. Later he regretted not having come clean; maybe it would have lessened the guilt of his obsession with Wimbledon.

******

The winter progressed, the garden looked untidy and uninviting; outings to the Downs or local parks were cold and windy. With no trips to London, life was almost back to normal. The reverberations of the Jonathan moment seldom made themselves felt, and then almost subliminally in occasional covert glances, in guarded words and slightly self-conscious care for each other. But as the green haze heralding spring wove its magic on trees and shrubs, and the sun began to gain a little strength, inviting them into the garden and parks again, even these hesitancies faded away and they relaxed once more.

Trevor threw himself into his work with increased energy, and Kate was able to think about taking an Open University course, untroubled by the nagging worries which had undermined her concentration for many months, putting all such ideas on hold. Together they planned a family holiday for that summer.

"How about camping in Brittany, somewhere by the sea?" Trevor spread a map out on the kitchen table. "The boys would love it."

"Let's ask them." Kate called them down and had to laugh at their enthusiastic response to the idea. "That's decided then!"

Weekends were busy too. The boys were in and out with friends, there were supper parties given and attended, and Trevor even managed to fit in an occasional game of golf. Kate's parents came to visit over Easter, and her older sister, who lived in the States, stayed for a few happy days.

Life was good.

Trevor surprised himself by singing as he cut the lawn and the three boys gambolled around him, helping to empty the grass collector into the compost bin, exclaiming at the proliferation of tiny worms revealed as they lifted its lid. He sent them on a snail hunt round the hostas with a jar of beer in which to give the leaf-spoilers a happy death, then set them to digging a corner of the garden for their very own vegetable patch.

Trevor looked up as Kate called them in for a drink and a biscuit. He saw she was smiling as she stood at the kitchen door watching them, the archetypal happy family of so many advertisements and sentimental films.

******

When the next summons to London for the resumption of the property negotiations came in June, Trevor barely hesitated before telling Kate he would be away for three days the following week, and the thought of Nicola and the child passed through his mind and out again sufficiently quickly for him to feel no nagging guilt.

"Shall I pack your bag as usual? How many shirts do you think you'll need? They say it's going to be very warm; do you have to wear long sleeved, or are short sleeves allowed these days?" As ever, Kate was organised and thoughtful.

"Still long sleeves, sadly, but it's cool in the office. But it would be great if you could fit in one or two short sleeve ones for the evenings. Thanks." Trevor gave her a quick kiss.

London was indeed hot and noisy but, closeted in Staffords' air-conditioned offices, Trevor could largely ignore it, only suffering for the short walk from his hotel. On the second day, there was an additional place set at the negotiating table.

"Who's the extra person?" Trevor asked the chair of the meeting.

"Horst. He'll be here in a minute or two, he's just sorting his papers. We want his viewpoints on the project at this stage so he's come over for a couple of days."

Trevor just nodded, but the news was not welcome. Horst walked in at that moment, shook hands all round and clapped Trevor on the back. "Good to see you, old man."

His disquiet was intensified when at lunchtime Horst suggested a stroll. Much as he respected Horst's business sense, Trevor found his playboy persona wearing; he was tired of the innuendo accompanying Horst's tales of office conquests and night club revels. As a balding, rather podgy forty-five-year-old, he was becoming an implausible Lothario.

However, Hanover Square offered leafy shade for a quick stretch of the legs and Trevor felt he could hardly refuse. After a couple of circuits of the square during which Trevor carefully kept the conversation general, Horst finally raised the subject of Nicola.

"Been in contact with Nicola? No? I heard through a friend at Capital that she was having marriage problems. Wonder if she'll try to get in contact with you again?" Trevor flinched mentally as

Horst nudged him in the ribs. "Wouldn't put it past her! She's not likely to stay single for long, knowing her. Still, she's got a kid now, apparently, and expensive tastes, so she won't find it so easy."

Trevor's heart sank as his curiosity rose again. "It's no good," he thought to himself. "I'll just have to nail this damned uncertainty and put it behind me once and for all."

He brought himself back to the present with an effort, deflected Horst's speculations with a shrug and turned the conversation to the development project. They walked back to the office, picking up sandwiches on the way, and went to separate offices to prepare for the afternoon session.

However, rather than starting work immediately on the legal papers, Trevor planned one more assault on Wimbledon, determining to set off immediately the meeting was over. He remembered that Horst had described Nicola as having expensive tastes, so decided his target would indeed be the big house which he had visited last time. This settled, and feeling resolute, he put his mind back onto the work in hand.

The afternoon meeting was tough, and it was nearly six before Trevor was able to get to the tube and make his way to Wimbledon. The train was miserably hot and crowded, too crowded to read the Evening Standard he had picked up, and he was glad to step out into the air again. Checking his phone he began the walk to St Mark's Road. Passing a little general shop, he went in and bought a bottle of water. It was well past seven by the time he stood outside the big house. He leant against the tree he had hidden behind before and scanned the house and drive. Again, there was no sign of life apart from the same silver Mercedes in the drive. He settled down to read the paper, looking up frequently to check on the house, but all was quiet.

It was eight before he suddenly realised what a fool he was still to be standing there. Surely any small children would be on their way to bed now, perhaps having their bedtime stories like his three back home, and there was no chance he would see his son. He would have to come back the next day, but much earlier. Damn.

He wrestled with this thought for a while, still leaning against the tree, then took out his mobile and called Kate.

"I'm terribly sorry, darling; I didn't get a chance to ring earlier to say good night to the boys." He took a deep breath. "I'm afraid I shan't be back in time for their stories tomorrow. This project is just not going as it should and I'll have to stay late again. I won't get back much before nine or ten." Her calm acceptance, trusting him so completely, made him feel as bad as he ever had, but he told himself once more that this was, absolutely, the last time. "Love you."

He switched the phone off, put it back in his pocket, and took a long sip of water before setting off back to the station. He dropped the paper in a bin and, on the train, leant back against the seat, his eyes closed, trying hard not to think about what he was doing.

The hotel provided a light meal which he washed down with most of a bottle of wine in the hope it would ease him into sleep. And indeed it did, but not before his mind had ranged over images of a charming, intelligent son who looked just like him alternating with the nightmare of Kate finding out about his shameful quest.

Chapter 11

Next day, as the morning meeting finished, Trevor made his apologies to the chairman.

"I'm sorry, but I shall have to miss this afternoon's session. There's a parents' meeting at my sons' school and I really need to be there." Turning to his colleagues, "Sorry to leave you gentlemen, but I don't think you need me present at this afternoon's meeting. We can have a quick discussion over lunch, and you can send me any questions at my Bristol office tomorrow."

Lunch over, he stuffed his papers into his briefcase and left, citing the unmissable parents' meeting – if only they knew, he thought grimly. Stopping only to pick up his overnight bag from the hotel, he set off for Wimbledon.

This time he was ensconced under the oak tree by 3pm, armed with the early edition of the evening paper and another bottle of water. He switched off his phone to avoid being distracted in his vigil.

He was soon rewarded by the sight of the smart woman he had seen before – definitely not Nicola – leaving the house by the front door and getting into the Mercedes. He was wondering again who she could be – Nicola's mother? A smart, expensive nanny? – as she drove slowly past him, giving him a searching look before speeding up and driving on.

He felt a tremor of anxiety, but dismissed it, his hopes rising that she was on her way to pick up Nicola's and his son from school and would soon be returning and putting his obsessive curiosity to rest. Guessing he had a few minutes to relax, he walked a few yards along the quiet leafy road and back, keeping to the shade of the trees which took the edge off the heat of the day and enhanced the fresh sweetness from the newly cut grass verges. Deciding he was not ideally dressed, he took off his jacket and tie, rolled the latter into a neat ball, put it into his overnight bag which he propped beside his briefcase under the oak, and hooked the jacket over his shoulder.

He was just finishing the easy crossword when he heard the shrill siren of a rapidly approaching police car. Looking up, he was surprised when it came to a halt beside him and two policemen climbed out and approached him.

"Excuse me, sir, but can you please tell us what you are doing here?" The larger, clearly senior officer did not sound friendly. The younger, slighter one was looking Trevor up and down, observing his attire, his briefcase and bag.

Trevor was stunned. What could he say? He blustered:

"Er, I'm just waiting for a friend." He didn't sound convincing even to himself. "It's someone I work with and I have some papers for her – him." He gestured towards his briefcase.

"Why wait out here?" The policeman clearly knew he was lying. "And on two days? I think you need to do better than that, sir."

"No, really, I'm not doing any harm. Just waiting." This sounded even more feeble. And the reference to 'two days' really shook him.

The younger policeman stepped uncomfortably close.

"We've had a report that you were here watching the house yesterday; quite some time you stood here before going away. Very suspicious, it looked. Casing the joint, were you? Not very clever about it." His tone was unpleasantly sarcastic. "And you were seen here before, back in the winter."

Trevor shrivelled inside, and his mind froze; he just couldn't come up with any ideas at all to explain his behaviour. It had never occurred to him that he himself had been watched.

The first policeman picked up Trevor's overnight bag.

"Mind if we look in here, sir?" He didn't wait for an answer and Trevor didn't bother to give one.

Was it to embarrass him or just bad luck that the bag fell open and deposited his washbag, underwear and carefully rolled-up tie onto the recently cut grass? The policeman's apology didn't sound sincere as he unzipped the washbag and poked around inside it before re-zipping it and handing it and the empty case to Trevor, who hurriedly scooped up his belongings and stuffed them inside.

The policeman turned his attention to the briefcase, though he stopped short of tipping all the papers out. He took his time absorbing their content, and to Trevor's disconcertment, made some notes in a small black book.

"Trevor Martin, is it, sir? Work for Staffords? What do they do, then?"

Trevor answered tersely: "Yes, I'm Trevor Martin and Staffords is a commercial property company. Why are you searching my bags? What are you looking for? What harm do you think I'm doing?" He tried to sound formal and assertive but knew that in his confusion and embarrassment he was only semi-coherent.

The men did not deign to answer immediately but looked at him speculatively.

"We need to frisk you, Mr Martin. Sir. If you don't mind. Otherwise we'll have to take you to the station. Please hold your arms out and stand with your legs apart."

Trevor's mortification was complete. Abjectly, he did as he was told, gritting his teeth as hands patted his pockets and ran the length of his arms. He cringed inwardly as the young man's hands ran down the inside of his legs. He wondered who was watching. Was it the same person who had reported his presence? Perhaps they were even now watching, gloating over his discomfort. A passing car slowed down and the driver turned to watch before driving on.

The policemen stepped back, faces impassive.

"Would you like to tell us what you are really doing here, sir?" The constant use of 'sir' rubbed in the indignity of his situation. "I'm afraid if you can't give us a good answer, we shall have to ask you to come back to the station with us."

Trevor was almost tearful as he faced his dilemma full on. Would he really have to tell these two strangers what he had told no-one else?

He hummed and hawed for a moment, buying time. If he declined to tell them the true story, what would happen next? Would they just keep him in the police station until he did tell them? Could he come up with a plausible story quickly enough to satisfy them? If he did refuse, would they let him go home tonight and would he be able to avoid any explanations to Kate? He couldn't imagine having to explain to her why he was late. And just suppose they contacted his office…

Trevor had no more resistance.

"I'm sorry. I'll tell you everything," he said in a very quiet voice. "But please can we sit in your car; it feels just too public here."

The two policemen looked at one another, and with the slightest incline of the head, the older one opened the rear door, motioned to Trevor to get in and slid in beside him. The young one got into the driving seat and swivelled round to look at him. The two watched him and waited.

"I'm almost too embarrassed to tell you," Trevor began. "Before I start, can you please reassure me that if I tell the truth, you won't contact either my wife or my company?"

"That depends," the older policeman's bulk seemed more intimidating in the confined space. The younger one got out his notebook and a pencil and raised a speculative eyebrow.

"Woman story is it, sir?"

Trevor found his tone and manner deeply offensive but decided he was not in a position to remonstrate.

"I suppose so," he sighed. "But that's not how I would put it." He paused, wondering where to start and how much to include. "Some years ago I did have an affair, yes. And I found out just last year that the woman, who used to be a colleague, had a baby which has to be mine, but she never told me about it. It was my wife who told me."

The policemen looked sideways at each other. Trevor could sense their prurient interest and determined to keep his account as bare as possible while still being convincing.

"She had found out about it through another colleague," he began before telling the sorry story as briefly as he could, finishing with his visit of the previous day. His voice trailed away as he tried to gauge their reaction.

"That's it. That's the truth. There is nothing else to tell." He leant back against the seat, his eyes closed in shame.

"Hmm. It's a pretty odd story, but not the sort of thing you'd be likely to make up, I accept that." The older man nodded to himself. "I think we can take your word on this; it fits with the observations of your behaviour. However, we'll do a check on your record, and I'm afraid we'll have to caution you. Jim will take the necessary details."

It somehow helped Trevor that at least one of his interrogators now had a name, and he gave his own name and home address calmly enough, relieved that this might be the end of the business. However, one burning question remained and, as Jim closed his notebook and tucked his pencil in the breast pocket of his uniform, Trevor ventured to raise it:

"Who reported me, and why did you react so strongly, sending two policemen, siren blazing? I would have thought I looked harmless enough."

"Can we tell him that, Mike?" Jim looked at his senior.

"Yes, I guess, at least in outline. You see up there," twisting in his seat and lowering his head to peer up and back through the side window. "On the lamp post. CCTV."

Trevor leant back to look through the rear window to where Mike was pointing. Sure enough, he could see a surveillance camera angled to give a view of the approach to the house. This degree of security had not reached the areas of Bristol he knew.

"Good heavens. But why? Who is this M. Bryant? The one my..." he searched for the right words, "...the one who married the mother of my son was just a commercial lawyer."

"Ah, that we can't tell you. He doesn't live here at the moment, in any case; the house is rented out. And the tenant, well, we're not going to tell you who he is either. But he's a very important bloke in a sensitive job, a potential target for some of our less savoury citizens. You really picked a bad place to hang around; lucky we didn't just shoot you, eh, Jim?" Mike chuckled.

Jim nodded. He and Mike seemed in no hurry and Trevor, weak with relief though he was, and desperate to get away from this nightmare, dared not push them too hard. However, after a few seconds of silence he ventured to suggest they might let him go.

"Well, Jim, do you think it's safe?" They were positively jocular now, and Trevor didn't like the suggestion of a smirk on Jim's face as he pretended to consider the matter.

"Do you think he's going to hang around other houses to find his son? Maybe try to get it together with the woman again? Would hate to think we had to take him in for stalking. Or has he learnt his lesson?"

"Oh, I don't think you need to worry about that!" Trevor spoke from the heart. "Please can I go now? I want to get back to Bristol in good time."

"Want a lift to the tube?"

Trevor wistfully but very briefly recalled boyhood dreams of riding in a police car, lights flashing and siren blazing. But he responded without hesitation.

“No, really, thanks all the same. The walk will give me time to go over my stupidity.”

His relief made him almost light-hearted and he found himself shaking hands with the two men before stepping out into the slightly cooler evening and picking up his bag and briefcase. Glancing at his watch, he saw that it was after four. As he turned to retrace his footsteps to the station, he glanced back at the house and suddenly realised he had not thought to look out for any arrivals while in the police car, before discovering it was definitely not the current Bryant home. He was none the wiser as to who lived there. He also realised, almost with relief, that this was perhaps just as well. Could he have stopped himself taking things any further if he had seen a small boy brought home in that Mercedes?

He sighed deeply, shook his head to clear it, and addressed himself out loud: “You fool. You utter and complete, shameful, bloody idiot,” and set off for the tube and the train home.

Chapter 12

Trevor collected his car and was home almost before he had finished rehearsing a cheerful, normal greeting – *so* unlike how he actually felt. He was surprised to see Ann's red Renault people carrier in the drive, parked behind Kate's blue hatchback.

He turned his key in the lock and opened the front door, calling out, "Hello, I'm home – not as late as I expected!"

The house was strangely quiet as he advanced into the hall: no sound from the playroom, no rush of feet to welcome him. As he bent to put down his briefcase and bag, the kitchen door opened and Ann appeared, followed by Charlie and Paul. The two boys burst into tears and rushed into his arms.

"Hey, you two, what's wrong?" Trevor hugged them to him, looking over their heads to Ann and raising his eyebrows.

Ann beckoned to him to come into the kitchen. He followed her, the two boys still holding his hands and sobbing, but making no attempt to tell him why.

"Sit down," she said quietly. "I'm afraid I have some bad news."

All thoughts of his recent trauma left him, and an awful internal chill caused him to collapse onto the nearest chair. He put his arms round the boys and looked up at Ann.

"What's happened? Kate…? James…? Where are they?" His voice was little more than a whisper.

"They're at the Children's Hospital, in A&E. There was an accident. James got hit by a car. We don't know how bad it is. Kate's with him."

Trevor covered his mouth with his hand, a wave of sickness engulfing him.

"Oh, my God. What happened?"

"Kate will tell you. Go now, I'll stay with the boys. They're in shock but they'll be OK. John came home early to look after our two. I'll call Kate and tell her you're on your way."

Trevor gave the boys a tearful hug and a kiss each. "Be brave, boys, Mummy and I will be back soon as we can."

"Thanks a million, Ann. I'll ring as soon as I know more," he called as he ran to the front door, grabbed his keys from the hall table, and sprinted to his car. Fortunately, the traffic was flowing fairly freely. He made no attempt to park correctly at the hospital but left the car in the '15 minutes only' section by the main entrance. He leapt from the car and sprinted the few yards to the entrance, realising as he ran that he had no idea where to go.

Surprised there was no reception desk, just the café and shop, he cast around anxiously until he saw the sign on the back wall for Emergency Admissions. Ignoring the lift, he took the stairs two at a time.

Another arrow pointed him along a corridor decorated with colourful images of butterflies and, at the end, he finally saw the reception desk. He hardly had time to pant out his name before the young nurse looked at him sympathetically and said, "Your son is in the receiving room. I'll take you in."

She came round the desk, led him across the corridor and opened the door into a brightly-lit room with four beds. Three were empty but James was in the far one, attached to a monitor of some sort, his red-gold hair contrastingly strongly with the starkly white pillow.

Kate was sitting on a chair beside the bed, her face pale and tear-streaked. She leapt to her feet as Trevor came in and turned to face him.

He moved forward to put his arms round her, but she backed away.

"They said you had left early for a parents' meeting." Kate looked at him coldly before turning back to the bed. "But thank God at least you're here now."

Trevor stood beside her.

"I'm very sorry. I'll explain later." He prayed that he would be able to come up with a good explanation, but his mind refused to face the problem just then. "But, for God's sake, tell me what happened. Is James all right? Is it very bad?"

"They don't know yet. He's unconscious – there may be internal bleeding, a couple of ribs are possibly broken – his shoulder may be broken too…" She stopped to take a breath. "We won't know how bad it is until he comes round – oh, Trevor, suppose he doesn't wake up!" This time she did let Trevor hold her, sobbing on his shoulder as he stroked her hair and kissed her forehead.

They stood quietly for a moment, looking down at the small boy, so vulnerable and pale. Looking around, Trevor saw another chair and pulled it up beside Kate's. They sat down and Trevor took her hand.

"Tell me everything."

At that moment, a nurse came in smiling and pulling a gurney. "We're going to take James for a scan then move him to a side ward. It won't take long. Would you like to wait in the room he'll be moving to?"

They both nodded.

"The nurse at the reception desk will take you there."

It was the same nurse as when Trevor had arrived. She led the way to a single room next to a small ward. It was simply furnished with a bed, two chairs and a bedside locker. There was a jug of water and a couple of glasses.

"Just wait here," she smiled and left the room.

Trevor poured a glass of water and offered it to Kate who shook her head. He put the glass back on the cupboard.

"So, tell me what happened," Trevor said urgently as they sat down side by side.

Kate took a deep breath.

"I'd fetched the boys home from school. It was a lovely afternoon and they wanted to play basketball in the front drive – I said they could. I was in the kitchen getting their tea ready when I heard an awful screeching of brakes."

She paused for a moment, her face re-registering the shock when she'd realised it was outside their house, that split second when she had been rooted to the spot.

"I ran outside. Charlie and Paul were standing at the end of the driveway screaming and screaming. There was no sign of James but there was a car half sideways across the road and a man was leaning on the bonnet. He looked up at me and I could see he was shaking.

"He kept saying, 'I'm so sorry, I'm so sorry. He just ran out, ran out…' He said he'd already called the ambulance and the police. I ran round the car and James was just to one side of the front wheel. There was a little blood on his face but otherwise he just looked asleep. I bent over him and could feel he was still breathing, but I didn't dare move him."

Trevor put his arms round her and she clung to him. He could feel her trembling.

"Charlie and Paul crept round to where I was kneeling and Paul said, 'Is he dead?'" Kate was unable to speak for a moment, then continued:

"The police arrived just then, and the man told them and me at the same time what had happened. The ball had run into the road and he swerved to avoid it, but James ran out without looking and there was nothing he could do… he swore he hadn't been driving fast.

"The ambulance arrived really quickly. Elizabeth next door came out and said she'd look after Charlie and Paul. I gave her Ann's number to get her to come and take over – I knew she would.

"I called you at your office from the ambulance. And they said… they said…" Kate turned away from him and her voice turned icy.

"They said you had left early to go to a parents' meeting. Where the hell were you? With bloody Nicola? I thought that was all over. Or are you fucking a different colleague this time?"

Trevor groaned and covered his face with his hands, unable to face his wife, overwhelmed by the shame and guilt of where he had actually been.

"Honestly, Kate, it's not what you think. I've not seen Nicola, I've not spoken to her – I haven't even contacted her." That at least was the truth. "And there's no-one else. Look, I promise I'll tell you tomorrow. I'm not proud of it – but it's partly your fault." That just slipped out and he could have kicked himself.

"My fault? *My fault*?" Kate's voice rose and she turned and pulled his hands from his face. "How dare you!"

Her slap took him by surprise. He reeled back, knocking over the chair he had been sitting on, which brought the glass of water on the side table crashing to the floor.

"You bastard, how dare you!" She was shouting now and backing away from him. The door opened and the same young nurse came in, taking in the broken glass and their angry stance.

"Mr and Mrs Martin, I know you're upset. This is all very stressful, but please think about the patients. And they will be bringing James back shortly; you don't want to upset him. Will you both be staying with him?"

Trevor overrode Kate's immediate, "No, I am," with:

"No, Kate. You must go back to Charlie and Paul. They're so worried and you're the best person to reassure them and explain. Ann will want to get home. You get the children fed and in bed, then I'll come home and take over. We can take it in turns from then. Take my car." He held out the key. "It's right by the main entrance."

Kate nodded, took the key, picked up her bag and, without looking at him, left the room. Trevor apologised to the nurse and, avoiding her eye, began ineffectually to gather up the pieces of broken glass. The nurse went out and was replaced by an orderly with a dustpan and mop, clearing the mess without comment.

Trevor sat down, perversely glad that Kate wasn't there, not knowing how he would cope with her anger and suspicion. It didn't seem the time to tell her about his need to see his other child.

He didn't know how long he had been there when the nurse and an orderly returned wheeling James on a gurney. He leapt to his feet as they transferred the silent boy carefully onto the bed and arranged the light blanket over him.

"How is he? What have you found out?"

The nurse smiled reassuringly.

"The doctor is hopeful that, apart from cracked ribs and a possibly broken shoulder, it's not too bad. There's no immediate danger. The best thing is that he sleeps through, and let's hope the concussion will wear off by the morning then we'll be able to get an idea of whether there's any other damage."

"Thank the Lord for that." Trevor breathed a sigh of relief and smiled at the nurse gratefully as she left the room. Moving to the bed he leant over to stroke the boy's forehead. He felt tearful from the shock, from the huge barrier he had so stupidly erected between himself and Kate, and from the embarrassment of his encounter with the police. He pulled the chair close to the bed, sat down, closed his eyes and tried to empty his mind. He couldn't cope with any more.

To his amazement he must have dozed, and he was roused by the same nurse tapping him on the shoulder.

"Your wife's trying to ring you but your phone's off. Please go into the corridor to use it." She went out again.

Trevor followed her out, fishing in his jacket pocket for his phone. He switched it on and pressed the button for home while glancing at his watch, surprised to see it was after 9pm. Kate answered immediately.

"The boys are in bed. Come home and when you're back, I'll come to the hospital." Her voice was emotionless.

He agreed and went back into the room, kissed James lightly and held his hand briefly, then left, explaining to the nurse that his wife would be back in half an hour or so.

He rang for a taxi and was lucky to get one almost immediately. He jumped in and leant back in the seat, his head against the rest. He sighed, wondering how he would get through the next days, barely registering the journey home. The taxi paid and dismissed, he found he couldn't go into the house without stopping to see exactly where the accident had happened. It was still light enough to see the tyre marks and he gave a brief prayer of thanks that the driver hadn't been going faster. He approached the front door with trepidation and turned the key in the lock.

Kate was just coming out of the kitchen as he entered the hall.

"The boys aren't asleep. Go up and say good night – and keep your phone on." She barely looked at him as she spoke. "I'll call if there's any news."

"Will you come back tonight?" Trevor hardly dared ask.

"No, I'll sleep in the chair in his room." And she was gone.

Chapter 13

Ignoring his bag and briefcase, still on the hall floor, Trevor ran quickly up the stairs. He was not surprised to find Charlie and Paul sitting up looking expectantly at the door as he went into their room. He sat down on Paul's bed, and Charlie came over to sit on his lap, something he rarely did now, considering it beneath a ten-year-old's dignity. He put his arms round both of them.

"Did Mummy tell you that James is just sleeping?"

They nodded.

"The nurse told me before I left that she hopes it's not too bad. We think he may have broken some ribs, and damaged his shoulder too, but they will heal – you'll have to be gentle with him for a while."

The boys nodded again. Then Paul ventured, almost whispering: "Was it our fault? Playing out there by ourselves?"

"No, of course not." Trevor was shocked that they might have felt to blame. "But it's better to lose a ball than to run out after it. You know we've always told you not to go into the road at all, but I guess in his excitement, James forgot." He held them tighter. "But it will all be all right, you'll see. Do you think you can go to sleep now?"

Charlie climbed off his lap and into his own bed; Paul slid down under the sheet. "We'll try."

"Good boys. Mummy is with James; I'll be downstairs if you need me." He kissed them both and tucked the sheets around them, folding their duvets at the end of the bed in case they were cold later. He blew them another kiss from the doorway then made his way downstairs, holding on to the banisters, feeling like an old man.

The kitchen was surprisingly tidy; Ann must have cleared it up, bless her. He opened the fridge, vaguely thinking he should eat, but immediately realised he wasn't hungry. He reached for a beer, then put it back knowing he needed something much stronger. "Whisky," he thought, and poured himself a generous measure in the first glass that came to hand. He had taken a sip when he was startled by the landline phone ringing. It took him a moment to find it on the dresser, under a pile of papers.

"It's Ann. Any news on James? John and I are so sorry. Glad I was able to help out."

"You're very kind; it was a huge relief to have you looking after the other two. James. Well, he's unconscious but…" and he went on to fill in what details he could. "Kate is staying with him tonight."

"I'll call again tomorrow. Let me know if I can help with Charlie and Paul. Will you be going to the office?"

"No, I'll stay home. But thanks again." He hung up and sat down with his drink, his elbows on the kitchen table. He ran his hand through his hair, got up and walked around the room, sat down again, finished his whisky and poured himself another. He tried to think about what he was going to tell Kate the next day, but his mind refused to focus, instead going back over the accident.

As he filled his glass for the third time he was reliving the scene in the hospital, groaning at the damage done by his stupidity. Did he dare ring Kate? He lifted the phone, then put it down again. Would the ring disturb James? He picked it up again and dialled Kate's mobile. She answered it immediately.

"I'm sorry. I love you." As he spoke, he became aware that the whisky had had more of an effect than he had realised. He made an effort to pull himself together. "How's James?"

"No change. Don't ring again. We'll talk tomorrow."

A fourth drink was the only appealing option. He carried it into the sitting room and slumped on the sofa, reached for the TV remote and flicked through the channels, then switched it off again and closed his eyes.

He was still there when the sun's early morning rays fell on his face, invoking a dream of summer holidays, tropical beaches and a laughing Kate beckoning him into the sea. But in fact it was Charlie who roused him, shaking his shoulder.

"Are you OK, Dad? Why are you still down here and in your clothes?"

It hurt to move his head but Trevor forced himself to smile.

"I guess I was too upset to get myself upstairs. What time is it?" He screwed his eyes up to read his watch. Half six. "How come you're down so early?"

"I woke up and couldn't stop thinking about James. I came to find you and got worried when you weren't in your bed. Can we go and see James? Please?"

"Is Paul awake too?"

Charlie shook his head.

"I think we should wait for Mummy to call, but let's have a shower while we wait. Want to shower with me?"

The boy forgot his fears for the moment at the thought of such a rare treat. He ran ahead, not seeing what an effort it cost his father to drag himself off the sofa. Paul emerged sleepily onto the landing in time to see Trevor hauling himself up the last few stairs.

"Coming to join us in the shower, old man?" Trevor forced a smile.

Paul nodded, grinning and all three of them stripped and stood together under the broad stream of deliciously hot water – though Trevor thought perhaps cold would have cleared his head faster. He wrapped the boys in the big warm bath towels and rubbed them dry, then himself. Dressing gowns on, they descended to the kitchen.

Can you two get breakfast ready if I do my coffee?”

They proudly prepared the table, selected their cereals and brought the milk jug from the fridge. Trevor breathed in the scent of the brewing coffee and began to feel he could face the day – until he realised he was very soon going to have to explain everything to Kate.

Chapter 14

Kate didn't expect to get any sleep as she sat beside James's bed, occasionally stroking his arm gently so as not to disturb him, listening for any change in his breathing. Her mind raced: again and again she relived the sickening moment when she had run from the house to find him almost under the wheels of the car. But then her thoughts switched to Trevor, the lie about the parents' evening and what it might mean.

Had he really been seeing Nicola again? His denial had been so forthright, she almost believed him. But if not Nicola, then who? Was he really a serial adulterer, in spite of his remorse and their recently happy times together? She could hardly bear the thought but it wouldn't go away, and she alternately raged and wept inside. How could she have been so deceived?

She went back in her mind over the recent months and his visits to London. Had there been anything suspicious? Had he been evasive? Surreptitious texting? No, he would have done that at the office or in the car. More tired than usual? No. Even racking her brains she couldn't think of any clues she might have missed. Then she remembered the children's Christmas party when he had reacted so badly to her talking to Jonathan; it seemed the whole business was still festering in his mind.

Reverting to the fiasco of their parting earlier that evening, she ran over the conversation – if that was what it had been. She puzzled over his words: "It's partly your fault." What could he have meant? She had no idea and, if she was honest, didn't fancy the process of finding out.

A tall black nurse with kind eyes came in and interrupted her thoughts. She checked James and gave Kate a reassuring smile.

"Why don't you try to get some sleep. You won't be disturbed for a few hours now as everything seems stable. I'm Nurse Julie. I'm on duty now and you can call me if there's a problem." She pointed to a bell pull.

Kate smiled back gratefully. In the early hours of the morning she did drift into sleep and was woken at six by the same nurse.

"Good morning, Mrs Martin. I'll just check James again. No problems in the night?"

"No. Thank you," Kate replied, watching the nurse as she checked the various monitors. The young boy stirred and Kate leant closer.

"What do you think?" she asked. "He looks the same to me, but can you see any difference?"

"His pulse and blood pressure are fine, and his breathing's normal. I've a good feeling. I reckon he's going to be just fine," the nurse said. "But you'll have to wait for the doctor to be sure."

Just then, James stirred again and slowly opened his eyes. "Mummy. Want Mummy." His voice was faint but the words were clear. He closed his eyes again.

"I'm right here darling." Kate leant over and kissed his forehead, then took his hand and squeezed it very gently. "I'm right here."

She looked up at the nurse, her eyes shining with hope. "That must be good, mustn't it? Doesn't it mean he's waking up?"

"I hope so, but the doctor will tell you more. Why don't you go and get something to eat? The hospital coffee shop is closed this early, unfortunately, but there's a vending machine. I'll be nearby so don't you worry."

Kate cast a glance at James, still unconscious – or maybe sleeping now, she hoped. "Yes, thanks. I'll be very quick in case he wakes again."

She picked up her handbag, followed the nurse out of the room and made her way downstairs. The reception and shop area felt very bare. There were only a few people there, mostly looking rather crumpled and as weary as she felt. There were two vending machines with drinks and snacks which offered some sustenance. After a moment's hesitation Kate bought a KitKat, thinking the chocolate would give her some energy, but she didn't fancy the fizzy drinks on offer. She ate half the KitKat, slipped the other half into her bag and returned to James.

Nurse Julie smiled at her as she passed the nursing station. "I'm off now. The doctors usually come round about ten so you've got a bit longer to wait, I'm afraid. I hope James will be fine."

Kate sat down beside James, leant forward and stroked his arm again. "I'm right here, darling. Don't worry." She looked for a sign he had heard but his eyes didn't flicker. Sighing, she looked at her watch. 6.30. Should she ring Trevor? She switched her phone on but a mixture of thoughtfulness – though "why shouldn't he suffer?" also passed through her mind – and the fact that there was nothing to tell him held her back. She decided to wait until the doctors had made their rounds. Putting the phone on vibrate she slipped it into her skirt pocket, yawned and leant back again.

She had no idea what time it was when she was roused by a strange jolting. It took her a moment to realise her phone was vibrating against her thigh. Casting a quick glance at James, still looking peaceful, she stepped out into the corridor and, rubbing her eyes, saw that the call was from Trevor.

Half-reluctantly, she answered the call with a simple "Hallo."

"What news?" Trevor also didn't attempt any niceties.

"None yet. He seemed to wake briefly and said 'Mummy' once, but nothing since. The lovely nurse on night duty was hopeful but we won't know more until the doctor comes round, maybe about nine," she looked at her watch, "in an hour or so. How are Charlie and Paul?"

"More or less OK. They were really upset last night, of course; they thought it was their fault for playing in the front garden without one of us there. But I hope I've reassured them. I let them get breakfast ready which cheered them up and they were really good." Trevor paused. "Do you think they should go to school? I won't go into work, of course. I've already left a message with the switchboard and called Virginia – my PA – at home to alert her before she left for the office."

"I'll come home now. I think school is probably a good idea – keep things normal, distract them from worrying. If I leave now I can be home in time to drive them as usual if you get them ready – remember, it's a games day, they'll need their games kit. It's all in their sports bags already – and hopefully I can still be back here before the doctor arrives."

"OK. What about you, are you OK, did you get any sleep?"

Kate heard him take a deep breath before he continued without giving her a chance to answer:

"I'm really sorry about last night. I promise it's not what you think. Anyway, I'll come down to the hospital as soon as you have taken over with the boys. Join me when you've dropped them at school then we'll both be there when the doctor comes."

"All right. I'll be home in twenty minutes." Kate ended the call and went back into James's room. She picked up her handbag and, casting a last look over her shoulder, left the room. She stopped at the nursing station to say she would be back in an hour or so, and her husband would be there sooner.

As she drove she suddenly remembered Trevor saying he had rung Virginia at home. Why would he have his PA's home number in his mobile? She felt another stab of pain at the idea that he might have embarked on another office romance. Did he have no self-control? Was she such an unattractive wife that she couldn't satisfy him?

It was rush hour but most of the traffic was coming down into the centre of Bristol so she was at the house in record time, barely noticing that it was a lovely morning, the sun having already burnt off any overnight mist.

As she opened the front door Trevor came into the hall, his car keys in his hand.

"Hello, darling." He moved to kiss her but she shrank away. His shoulders drooped and he failed to meet her eye. He looked grey and tired.

He looks like a defeated man, Kate thought. Has he really got an explanation?

Charlie and Paul, neatly dressed in their grey school shorts and crisp white shirts, ran out of the kitchen into her arms and she hugged them both tightly.

"Hallo, darlings. Are you all OK and ready for school? Have you got your games kit?"

"Do we have to go to school? Can't we come with you to see James? I'm sure he'd like to see us." Paul looked up at her optimistically. Charlie nodded in agreement.

"No, he's still asleep and we don't want to disturb him. It's best you go to school; it'll help the time pass faster until we come home this evening. Did Daddy tell you the nurse said she thinks he'll be OK?"

The boys nodded but looked only partly reassured.

"I'll just dash upstairs to shower and change; I slept in these clothes last night and feel really grotty. I promise I'll be really quick and you won't be late for school. Trevor, you go straight to the hospital now in case the doctor comes round early."

Trevor nodded, gave the boys a hug and a kiss and left. The boys followed Kate upstairs, asking about James, and squatted on the floor outside her bathroom until she emerged a few minutes later, wrapped in her big white towel. She dressed quickly in a cotton skirt and T-shirt, guessing it would be a very warm day. She almost didn't bother with any make-up but decided that a dash of lipstick and a touch of eyeshadow would make her feel more able to face the day and what it might bring.

Feeling much refreshed, Kate clapped her hands at the boys:

“Let’s go. We can talk in the car.”

Chapter 15

Kate drove slowly out of the drive, horribly aware of what had happened there the night before.

"So, did Ann and Daddy look after you all right?" Kate wanted to keep the conversation away from the accident itself. "What did you have for supper?"

"Ann made us egg and chips – yummy!" Paul was quick to answer. "She let us have lots of ketchup, more than you do!"

"Sssh. She said not to tell." Charlie poked his brother in the ribs.

"It's OK," laughed Kate. "Just this once – don't expect it every time now." She judged there was just time to touch on James and the accident without going into details before they pulled up at the school gates and the boys would be drawn into pre-school games. "I'm going straight to the hospital to join Daddy and see the doctor. James slept all last night so maybe he'll wake up soon. Shall I give him your love?"

"Yes, lots!" was the responding chorus.

Once parked at the school's designated stopping place, she hugged the boys again and waved them into the playground where they were soon swept up by their friends. Once they were happily engaged, she looked round for the member of staff on duty and went up to her.

"Good morning. I'm Charlie and Paul Martin's mother. The staff need to know that their younger brother was in a car accident last night and is in hospital. We've told the boys not to worry, that it shouldn't be too bad, but I thought I should alert you in case they get upset during the day. Please will you pass on the message to their class teachers. I have to get back to the hospital or I would come in myself."

"I'm really sorry to hear that, Mrs Martin. Of course I'll tell them. I do hope the little one is OK."

Kate nodded her thanks and returned to the car. She set off towards the hospital but the traffic was bad and it was slow progress. As she sat in yet another long traffic light queue, she started thinking about Trevor. Did she really believe him? Or was this the last straw? Could she bear to have him in the house? Could she cope without him? She felt a sudden chill. Had it really come to that?

Preoccupied with her thoughts, she was almost surprised to find she had arrived at the hospital. The car park wasn't full and she quickly found a space and made her way inside, still not sure what she was going to say, or even what she really felt. Her desire to see James conflicted with her confusion about Trevor, and her footsteps dragged as she approached his room. She took a deep breath, knocked lightly, turned the door handle and went in.

"Darling – it's OK, it's OK! He woke up! He's going to be fine," Trevor half whispered, throwing his arms around her and holding her tight, not giving her a chance to resist. "I didn't ring as I knew you would be in the car and here very soon. He's just fallen asleep again."

Kate extricated herself from his embrace, all worries about Trevor banished as she went over to the bed and looked down at James. She brushed his forehead lightly with her lips then stood back, tears of relief flowing gently. Wiping her eyes, she turned to Trevor.

"How do you know he's OK? Won't they have to wait and do more tests?"

"Apparently not. The doctor came round early, about half an hour ago, and James woke while he was here. He was quite lucid: he recognised me instantly and could answer all the doctor's questions. The monitors show everything as 'normal' so the doctor said he thinks there's nothing except maybe a couple of broken ribs which they'll know about for sure when they've done some X-rays, plus mild concussion. His shoulder's bruised too, must be from how he fell."

"Thank God for that." Kate sat down suddenly in the chair by James's bed. "What happens now? I guess he can't come home yet."

"The doctor didn't say much except that children's bones heal very quickly and there's nothing to worry about. He'll have to stay here until they're sure the concussion has worn off, though, but I don't know if they'll move him to a children's ward or keep him here."

"Let's ask the nurse when she comes round again. She'll probably know. In fact, I'll go and see if she's at the nursing station." Kate stood and left the room.

Trevor sat in the just-vacated chair and tried to imagine telling Kate the full story here, in front of James who might wake at any minute, but decided it would be just too difficult.

Kate returned a few moments later.

"The nurse said they will probably move him to a children's ward later today, but she didn't know when. Said we can stay with him meanwhile."

She moved the other chair to the opposite side of the bed and sat down, not looking at Trevor. The silence was uncomfortable. After a few minutes, the tension was relieved by James waking and looking round at them.

"Hello, Mummy. Daddy says I'm going to be better soon. When can I go back to school?"

"Yes, darling, isn't that wonderful! But no school just yet, you'll be uncomfortable for a few days at least as the bones have got to heal – no rough games!" Kate smiled happily at his return to normality.

"But it'll be boring at home all day without Charlie and Paul."

Kate smiled. “Maybe we could ask Paul if you could play with his fort sometimes, and we can read lots of books together. I might even let you watch some television!”

“Really?” James started to sit up in anticipation but screamed as pain kicked in and he fell back on his pillows.

Trevor and Kate both leapt to soothe him as he sobbed. “That hurt. Will it hurt for a long time?”

“Let’s hope not,” Trevor reassured him, “but the doctor will tell us more next time he comes. I’ll ask the nurse if we can get some painkillers for you.” He got up and left the room, returning a few minutes later with the news that they would again have to wait for the doctor.

“Kate, why don’t you go home and rest for a while. You probably didn’t get much sleep last night.” He forbore to mention his drunken sleep on the sofa. “I can stay. Virginia rang to say there’s nothing urgent at the office so James and I won’t be interrupted.”

“But I’ve only just got here,” she remonstrated.

“You’ve probably got things to do at home, and, if I’m honest, it’s quite a treat for me to have time just with James, and I’ve nothing particular to do at home. I cut the grass at the weekend and the garden’s quite tidy. The office can call my mobile if anything important turns up. James and I can tell each other silly stories when he’s awake, can’t we young man?”

James smiled at being called ‘young man’, then closed his eyes and drifted into sleep again.

With a slight sigh, Kate picked up her bag, dropped a light kiss on James’s forehead and left the room without a word.

Chapter 16

Walking back to the car, Kate felt shunned. Why was Trevor so insistent she should go home? Was he hiding something again? Angrily refusing to think about it right then, she retrieved the car and drove home.

The house felt unusually empty, different from a normal day. She wandered through the downstairs rooms, wondering whether to go to bed or to keep busy, though she doubted she would sleep with so much going around in her head. In the kitchen, she remembered an old cookery book which opened with the injunction always to put the kettle on first. Even though she had no inclination to cook right then, perhaps she would make a hot drink. At least it was something positive to do. Tea was marginally more appealing than coffee. The kettle boiled quickly and, clasping a mug of strong tea in both hands, she sat at the kitchen table. She glanced at the copy of The Week which lay on the table but couldn't concentrate enough to take in the words.

"It's no good, I just have to keep busy," she said out loud, putting down the barely touched tea. Remembering that there was a pile of washing in the laundry room and some still in the basket in their bedroom, she stood up and set off for the stairs. Passing through the hall, she noticed Trevor's overnight bag lying on the hall floor where he had dropped it the evening before and she made a mental note to pick it up on her way back downstairs.

In her bedroom, she looked at herself in the mirror, wondering how much the trauma of the past hours would show in her face, and was surprised how normal she looked, not even dark circles under her eyes. She gathered the dirty clothes from the basket and went to check the boys' bathroom and bedrooms. The latter were remarkably neat. Maybe Ann had tidied up before leaving, she thought, thankful for such a thoughtful friend.

Clasping the clothes to her, she negotiated the stairs and picked up Trevor's bag as she passed. In the laundry room, she sorted the clothes into piles then tipped the contents of the bag carefully onto the work surface. The shirts she put in with the other light colours, then picked up his underpants. As she moved to put them in the hot wash pile, she suddenly noticed that there were grass cuttings clinging to them.

She paused, her hand in mid-air. Grass, in his underwear? How on earth did… She froze. A wave of anger swept through her. The lying, deceiving bastard. All that sweet talk over the last months, then this. Her relief at James's recovery was buried under the certainty that she could no longer believe a word Trevor said, that things had gone beyond patching up. Her mind went back to that excruciating counselling session – perhaps it was her turn to demand a divorce.

The realisation of what it would mean to them as a family – the effect on the children, the family's hopes and plans for the future – overwhelmed her. She felt sick. Mechanically, she loaded the shirts into the machine, set the programme, added the washing powder and pressed 'start'. Then, rolling the grassy underpants into a ball, she returned to the kitchen, dumped them on the table, and sat staring at them without seeing, her mind refusing to work.

Kate had no idea how long she had been sitting there when she was startled by the house phone ringing. Forcing herself to come back to the present, she reached behind and lifted the handset.

"Hallo." She couldn't put any life into her voice.

"Hi, it's Ann. Are you OK? You don't sound right. Is it bad news about James, is he OK?"

"No, no James is going to be fine. He woke properly this morning. Trevor is with him." Just the mention of his name was enough to break her and the tears came, her shoulders shaking with the sobs.

"What is it, Kate? What's happened?"

Kate was unable to answer. She dropped the phone back into its rest, laid her head on her arms and gave way to the tears. Eventually, exhausted, she fell asleep where she was.

She was woken by an arm circling her shoulders and the warmth of a body beside her. Lifting her head, she found Ann had pulled a chair up beside her and was holding her as if she was a child.

"I was so worried, you sounded so awful. I came straight round and let myself in. Can you tell me what's wrong? Are you ill?"

Kate shook her head.

"What else – surely Trevor's not ill?"

Again Kate shook her head but forced out: "But it is about Trevor..."

"Look, if it's that bad, you have to talk to someone, surely better me who's known you since forever, who was there the day you met him. You know you can trust me with anything. Anything."

"Bless you, Ann. But I don't know... it's too hard... Oh, Ann, I'm not sure I can. It's..."

Kate pulled herself up and took a deep breath. Unable yet to look directly at Ann, she clenched her fists and stared into the distance.

"It is about Trevor. He's having another affair." There, it was out.

Ann couldn't hide her shock at the revelation.

"Oh, Kate, I don't know what to say. You've seemed so happy together. And *another* affair? You never mentioned anything like that before. But how did you find out – and last night of all times?"

Kate pointed at the underpants still sitting on the kitchen table. "How does a man get grass clippings in his underwear, tell me that."

Ann had to hide a smile at the strangeness of the evidence.

Kate's voice turned cold. "Trevor was working in London for a few days so I rang the office there from the ambulance to tell him about James and the accident. They said he had left early to go to a parents' evening, but he had told me he would be working late."

"That does sound bad, I admit," said Ann sadly. "But *another* affair, when was the first? You never said anything about it, not a hint."

"No, I kept quiet about it, didn't even tell Trevor I knew, in the hope it would fade away – and I thought it had. It was five or six years ago, a woman called Nicola from his old company. He's been going to London quite a lot recently, says there's a big new project. It all fits..." Kate's voice trembled.

Ann took Kate's hands in hers. "Oh, dear, I am so sorry. I know it looks dreadful, but maybe, just maybe, it's not as bad as you think."

"But what do I do, what do I say, how can I ever believe him again? James will still need lots of support and the other two are pretty upset. I don't see how I can just throw Trevor out, it would be too much for them all to cope with – never mind me. Until yesterday, I thought we were fine, in spite of..." Here she paused again, realising that she was about to embark on their showdown about James.

"Actually, it's more complicated." Kate straightened up and at last looked directly at Ann. Taking a couple of tissues from the box on the dresser behind her, she wiped her eyes and blew her nose. "I'd better tell you the whole story. I've never told anyone before, but I think I need to now." She paused. "Promise you won't say anything, even to John."

Ann nodded. "I promise."

"Have you noticed that James doesn't look like either of us – he has red hair for a start?"

Ann nodded again.

"Well, Trevor isn't his father. It's... No, you don't need to know. But a couple of years or so ago, Trevor began to get very cold and strange and we were having a hard time, so last year I arranged a counselling session. God, it was horrible. In front of the counsellor – a woman we'd never met before – he announced that he knew James was not his son, that he knew who the father was, and wanted a divorce."

Ann was silent for a moment, taking it all in. "So how did you get over that? You've seemed really comfortable together recently."

Kate recounted the story of that traumatic period: the drunken one-night stand, how a few days after the counselling session she had confronted Trevor with her knowledge of his own affair, how contrite he had been, and that they had tacitly agreed to forgive each other. She hesitated over telling Ann about Trevor's child by Nicola and decided not to.

"It took a while for things to settle down, for us to trust one another and be comfortable again, but it really was working. I had relaxed. Until last night and his lie about the parents' meeting."

"What did you say to Trevor when he turned up at the hospital? It must have been horrible, dealing with that and James's accident."

"I accused him of still seeing Nicola. He swore that he wasn't and that he'd not seen her since the affair ended round about the time James was born. So I said who was it then, he said no-one and – this was the last straw – he said it was partly my fault!"

“All this in the hospital room? With James there?” Ann was shocked.

“Not exactly. It was while James was taken away for a scan. We calmed down when he came back and Trevor came home while I stayed overnight. Then I came home while he stayed. I couldn’t sleep, even though I was tired, so I decided to do the washing and that’s when I found the underpants, in his overnight bag.”

“What are you going to do now?” Ann looked concerned.

“I don’t know, I just don’t know, but I really don’t think I can face being here with Trevor.”

At that moment the phone rang showing Trevor’s mobile number. Kate picked it up and held it away from her ear.

“Darling, good news! The doctor’s been round, said the X-rays showed two ribs are cracked, not actually broken. There’s bruising of course, and the concussion but even that’s wearing off. James has been talking to me quite normally. Isn’t that wonderful!”

“Yes.” Kate’s response was terse, but Trevor continued as if he hadn’t noticed.

“The doctor says he can even come home later today. I’ll call when we’re given the green light. Hope you slept. Love you. Bye.”

Kate and Ann looked at each other.

“He’s either a very good actor, or a cold-hearted bastard,” was Ann’s immediate comment.

“So, what do I do? Where to begin, how to avoid a shouting match?” She grinned suddenly. “I didn’t tell you that I hit him in the hospital when he said it was partly my fault. I didn’t know I had it in me! Anyway, right now I can’t imagine living with him and pretending all’s well in front of the boys. At least I can sleep in the spare room, saying I need to keep an eye on James.

“The idea of divorce just fills me with horror – the effect on the boys, especially poor James if he ever discovers he was the reason for the first problem – let alone that Trevor is not his real father. It all goes round and round in my head and I get nowhere. I must be around to look after James. The others will have to be very careful with him until his ribs heal." Kate's head was lowered as she spoke as if trying to disappear from the scene.

Ann thought for a moment. "Then how about taking James to stay with your parents for a few days, as soon as he's allowed home? You could say he needed peace and quiet and no boisterous brothers around. Trevor could surely get a few days' leave in the circumstances to look after Charlie and Paul. It would give you time to think – and make it clear to Trevor that you didn't want him around."

Kate's face lifted. "That's a very good idea, thanks Ann. They'd love it and I wouldn't have to tell them the real reason. I expect I can get through tonight somehow and take him there tomorrow. It's Thursday today, Trevor can take tomorrow off – the office will be very understanding – then it's the weekend so he will be home anyway. I can't think beyond that yet."

Kate gave Ann a hug. "You're a good friend. Thank you for coming round, I don't know how I'd have coped without you. It's been such a relief to talk about it to someone who cares, after bottling so much up for so long. How about a cup of tea? Or something stronger after this bombshell?"

Ann laughed. "No, tea would be fine. I must get home soon and tidy up and do something about my lot's supper. There's a couple of hours before the boys get out of school."

Kate refilled the kettle and set out mugs and biscuits. "I don't know about you, but I'm suddenly very hungry – didn't get any dinner last night, the hospital café was closed, and anyway I really didn't feel like breakfast."

They were quietly enjoying the tea, carefully avoiding the Trevor subject, when Kate suddenly jumped up.

"Blast! I forgot about the shirts sitting in the washing machine. Now they'll be really creased and hard to iron. Damn." Then she smiled. "I told myself I needed to keep busy!"

Ann stood too. "I'll be going now. Don't hesitate to call me any time; you know I'll be thinking of you." She held Kate close, kissed her on both cheeks, retrieved her handbag, waved goodbye and left.

Kate sat down again, picked up the phone and dialled her parents.

"Hallo, Mummy, how are things with you both?"

"Fine dear, and with you? How are the boys?"

"Please don't be alarmed, it's not too serious, but James was hit by a car yesterday. He ran into the street chasing a ball."

"Good heavens. Is he really all right? How did it happen? Was he hurt?" Mrs Adamson reacted as any mother or grandmother would, her words tumbling over themselves.

"The ambulance came and took him to the Children's Hospital. Trevor and I took turns to be with him. He called a few minutes ago to say the concussion has worn off and the doctor says he thinks there's no internal bleeding, but James does have a couple of cracked ribs. He can come home later today."

"Thank goodness for that. You must have been so worried. I'm glad you didn't tell us before." She raised her voice. "Geoffrey, it's Kate on the phone. James has had an accident but he's going to be OK."

Kate could hear her father in the background. Another "thank heavens."

"But Mummy, can I ask you a favour? James is going to need to be quiet for a few days. I wondered if we might come and stay with you, just James and me, until he's recovered a bit. I would worry at home in case Charlie and Paul were a bit too rumbustious for him."

"Of course, darling. When will you come? Today?"

"No, I think that would be too much for James, and the others would feel cheated if they couldn't spend a little time with him. They felt really bad about playing basketball in the drive without one of us there. If it's OK with you, I'll come tomorrow morning."

"No problem. I'll lay in some of his favourite food – and some chocolate biscuits. Apart from the accident, it will be lovely to have you with us for a few days, won't it Geoffrey?"

"Of course, love to have you. I'm very fond of James – the others too, of course – and I'll enjoy reading to him and playing games. Never enough time for that when you all come." Her father must have picked up the extension.

"Oh, dear, I've just had a thought." It was Mrs Adamson again. "What about the dogs? They can be a bit boisterous."

"I hadn't thought of that." Kate's spirits dropped momentarily. "But I'm sure we can keep them apart most of the time. We'll worry about that when we're with you."

"If you're sure, dear. I'll go and make the beds right away. See you tomorrow – let us know what time to expect you."

"Will do. Lots of love, and thank you." Kate replaced the phone and suddenly felt much better for having taken one positive step.

Chapter 17

Now she felt stronger and more in control, Kate decided to ring Trevor but his phone was engaged, which did nothing to assuage her fears and anger. Trying again five minutes later she was relieved when he answered almost straight away.

"I rang just now but you were on the phone." She tried not to sound too accusing.

"Yes, I was talking to Virginia, telling her I wouldn't be in for the rest of this week and checking that there were no urgent messages for me. I've only just hung up and was still in the corridor which is why I could answer so quickly."

"Oh." She paused, registering it was his PA he had been talking to. "Is James awake? Do you have any idea what time you'll be able to bring him home?"

"James is dozing. He sleeps quite a lot but is just fine when he's awake. We haven't been told a time yet, but I did ask if he would need an ambulance and they said no. They will put his arm in a sling and bandage his ribs, but my car will be fine."

"It's two o'clock now and I have to get Charlie and Paul from school at 3.30. See if you can arrange to come home after five, so I'll have had time to give them tea and for Charlie to do his homework if he has any." Kate was about to hang up when she had a sudden thought. "Has James had anything to eat?"

"They gave him some biscuits and a glass of milk at lunchtime. He enjoyed them a lot and asked for more!" Trevor laughed. "It was hard to believe there was anything wrong with him."

"Call me when you know more." Kate hung up, not wanting to prolong the conversation.

She had barely put the phone down when it rang again.

"Yes?"

"Kate, why are you being so short with me? What's wrong?"

Kate couldn't think quickly how to respond; she couldn't imagine how to have the conversation – one she knew she could not postpone for long – on the phone.

"Kate, are you still there?"

"Yes. Look, I'm not sure this is the time to explain. We'll talk tonight. Call me again when you know what time you'll be coming home. I'll go and get his room ready and think about food for you all." And she hung up.

Kate found she was trembling as she put the phone down. How was she going to get through the afternoon and behave normally with the children, be apparently relaxed in front of them and Trevor? She needed time to think about confronting him; it was almost like a replay of that awful first confrontation when she had confessed to her affair and told Trevor she had known about his. That had ended well, but this one wouldn't, she was sure.

There was an hour before she had to fetch the boys. Seeing the offending underpants were still on the table, after a moment's thought she took them into the laundry room and put them on one side. Moving upstairs, she tidied Charlie and Paul's room, taking care to make it look especially welcoming, putting their favourite books on the pillows.

Across the passage, Kate stood a few moments in James's room, thinking with relief that, although there were cracked bones, it could have been very, very much worse. Knowing James would still be in pain, she made the bed with just a sheet, not tucked in so that he could turn more easily, and folded the light duvet at the end of the bed. She put his favourite soft toy half under the sheet so that the bear's eyes were peeping cheekily over the top.

She went across the landing to her and Trevor's room to freshen up before the school run. The sight of their big, comfortable double bed was painful so she made herself go straight to the bathroom where she splashed her face with cold water and combed her hair aggressively before putting on some lipstick and eyeshadow and returning downstairs.

Tending to the boys' rooms, then going into hers, brought the impending rupture to the fore and she felt both tearful and cold as she thought about breaking the news to Trevor and the boys. How would they react? How would she cope with the coming storm? It was hard to believe it was less than two days since she had felt secure and happy, that they had been looking forward to the camping holiday in France. What would the summer holidays be like now?

Kate broke from her reverie and went back downstairs to deal with the washing. A sudden stab of conscience pricked her; unless Trevor had rung them and not told her, his parents knew nothing of the accident. Looking at her watch, she calculated she just had time to call them.

There were several rings before the phone was picked up. "Hello?"

"Hello, Susan? It's Kate. How are you?"

"Hello dear, nice to hear from you. Sorry I was slow answering but I was in the garden. It's been so warm, everything needs watering."

"I can imagine. Has Trevor rung?"

"No, not recently, naughty boy."

"Well, I thought I ought to tell you – and please don't worry, it's not too bad – James was hit by a car yesterday when he ran into the road chasing a ball. Luckily, the car wasn't going fast but it was really scary. He's in hospital and they've done lots of tests. By a miracle it seems there's no serious damage, just some cracked ribs. He had concussion too, but that's worn off quite quickly and he's coming home this afternoon."

"Oh, poor little mite. Can we come to see him?"

"Actually, I was a bit worried about Charlie and Paul being a bit too boisterous, so I've arranged to take him to my parents tomorrow. I don't know how long we'll stay – not too long, I hope, just until he's more comfortable. But as soon as he's home you must come over."

"Of course, but do give him lots of love from us, won't you. I was going to say give him a hug, but maybe that's not a good idea!" Susan chuckled. "Thanks for ringing and do keep us up to date with progress. Who's going to look after the other two?"

"Trevor is going to take tomorrow off, and maybe do some work from home next week. Why don't you call him tomorrow? Suggest you come to us over the weekend, or he could bring the boys to see you. They always love visiting you – something to do with you spoiling them something rotten! Sorry, Susan, I must dash, got to pick them up from school. Will you tell John for me? Love to you both. Bye."

"I understand, will do. Bye, dear, thanks for calling."

Kate detected a note of disappointment that the call had been so brief.

By then it was definitely time to fetch Charlie and Paul. She quickly checked the kitchen then went to her car and drove the half-mile to the school. Leaving the car in the designated parking area, she walked the few yards to the gates. There were only a few minutes to wait before the joyful crowd of children tumbled out, chattering, looking for their mother or, in a few cases, their father or au pair. Charlie and Paul were among them, hair tousled, cheeks glowing, dragging their sports bags behind them.

As they walked to the car, it was a race to share the news of their day, that Charlie had won the 200m race, that Paul had got a star for getting all his sums right. But then they remembered.

"How's James?"

"Is he coming home soon?"

"Will his broken bones stick out?" That last one from Paul.

Kate couldn't help laughing. "No, of course they won't. But he is coming home today, I don't know exactly when. Daddy'll ring when he knows."

"Goody. I want to ask James where it hurts." Paul again.

"You will have to be gentle with him, but I've arranged to go with him to Granny and Grandpa's for a few days so he can be quiet and rest. Daddy will look after you two, maybe take you swimming if the weather stays good, or to visit Nan and Pops. James would be sad if he had to stay at home while you had fun."

The boys' faces showed their mixed feelings on this. Did swimming with Daddy measure up to a visit to their other grandparents in their big house and garden – and the dogs? They were unusually silent for the rest of the short drive home.

"OK, you two," as she turned into the drive and stopped outside the front door. "Don't just drop your bags in the hall! Go up and put your sports clothes in the wash, then there might just be some chocolate biscuits for tea when you come down. Oh, and wash your hands too."

Obediently, the boys followed her into the house and disappeared upstairs. In the kitchen, Kate opened a packet of their favourite chocolate chip cookies, put two on each plate and poured two glasses of milk. The thundering of hungry footsteps and loud thump as they jumped the last few steps alerted her and she forced a welcoming smile.

"Yum, thanks, Mum," they said in unison as they tucked in.

"Have you got any homework tonight?"

"I haven't," said Charlie gleefully.

"What about you, Paul?"

"Miss Taylor said we should bring in a flower from the garden, then we can see how many different sorts there are, and what's special about them."

"What a nice idea! Let's go and pick one together when you've finished."

"Mummy, if I ask you very nicely, please can I have another biscuit? I'm so hungry."

"Honestly, Charlie, I think you've got hollow legs," Kate laughed. "But it's going to be early supper tonight because of James, so no." But as she spoke she realised she hadn't given supper a moment's thought. Don't panic, she thought to herself while continuing to smile at the boys and collect their plates and glasses. Surely there's something in the freezer I can use.

"It's still sunny so let's go out and pick that flower for you, Paul. Coming too, Charlie?"

"Yes. I can think which one I would choose if it was me."

The three of them emerged into the late afternoon sun which was still lighting most of the garden. Kate and Trevor had both learnt from their gardening fathers the value of a back garden which caught the afternoon sun, and made it one of their criteria when choosing the house.

While the two boys roamed the garden, stopping to sniff the flowers and to feel their leaves, Kate took her secateurs from the kitchen windowsill and went to Trevor's beloved rose bed, stooping to take in the scent of each variety. She cut half a dozen sweet-smelling blooms and formed them into a colourful bouquet.

"Smell these, boys," she invited, offering the bunch.

"Mmmm, a bit pongy," said Paul, wrinkling his nose.

"Nice," said the more discerning Charlie.

"Have you decided which flower you want to take tomorrow, Paul?"

"Yes," pointing to a scarlet geranium in a terracotta pot by the French windows.

"Let's take one with a nice long stem. You don't need to cut geraniums; if you're careful you can break them off where they join a main stem. Watch." Kate pulled off a showy flower head

and handed it to Paul. "We'll put it in water and it will be fine tomorrow. Charlie, which one did you pick out?"

He led them to the other side of the garden where a clump of agapanthus was in full bloom, their blue petals sharp in the light shade of the Judas tree. "I like those, and you don't see as many of them as roses round here. I bet no-one takes one of those to school."

"You're probably right, but I guess not many will think of geraniums either. Both great choices. Well done. Now amuse yourselves for a bit while I think about supper."

"Race you to the tree house!" shouted Paul and set off down the garden.

Watching them clamber up the makeshift ladder into the clever structure which Trevor had built for them in the old oak tree at the end of the garden brought another pang. Trevor was not just a good cook and successful lawyer, but handy too, his practical skills maybe learnt from his builder father. Kate shook her head in sadness at what the children and she were going to lose.

Chapter 18

Kate's brain had been working quietly away to solve the supper problem and led her to the chest freezer which lived in the garage. The debate about whether to bother with something so large had been solved with the gifts of fruit and vegetables from parents' gardens. Opening it she gazed at the contents. Right, she thought, spaghetti Bolognese, then stewed plums and ice cream. Bound to go down well. She extracted a packet of mince and a bag of her father-in-law's plums. Kate's parents had taught her to label every package with both contents and dates. Types of food neatly separated. She felt both amused and rather smug when her friends talked of UFOs – Unidentified Freezing Objects – in their freezers.

There were several packets of pasta in the kitchen cupboard. Taking down one of spaghetti, she paused. Eating spaghetti might be a bit awkward with the sore ribs. OK, penne Bolognese tonight.

Glancing at her watch she saw it was nearly 5.30. Rapidly, she checked on the plums – done. She made the Bolognese sauce deciding that heating it all through would take no longer than cooking the pasta. Finally, she laid the kitchen table, placing the bowl of roses in the centre. Wiping her hands and pushing her hair back off her face, she stood back, relieved that the flurry of activity had stopped her worrying thoughts. Before they could start again, the boys came in from the garden laughing and joshing each other.

"Mmmm, nice smell, Mum. What's for supper?" Charlie went over to the stove and checked the pan. "Spaghetti Bolognese, yummy!"

"Is there a pud?" asked Paul hopefully.

"Yes, plums and ice cream," smiled Kate, knowing they would be pleased. "But it's penne Bolognese 'cos I thought it would be easier for James to eat. And look, Paul, I've put your geranium in a jam jar on the bookcase there for tomorrow. Don't forget it!"

"I won't. Isn't it a lovely colour!"

It was true, the scarlet petals and bright green leaves really stood out against the white walls of the kitchen, and echoed the colours in the flower picture above the bookcase, a painting she and Trevor had found at a charity sale a couple of years before.

"Now, would you like to watch the pirate film we recorded while we wait for Daddy?"

There was no mistaking their enthusiasm as the two boys settled themselves on the floor with their backs against the sofa as Kate switched on the TV and found the film. They were soon immersed in it and Kate retreated upstairs to comb her hair. She debated again whether to put on lipstick and eyeshadow; on the one hand she felt Trevor didn't deserve it, but on the other it would give her confidence a boost to know she looked good. The need for confidence won and, as she checked the finished effect in the mirror, she was glad she had bothered.

Passing through the hall on her way back to the kitchen, her eye was caught by a flash of light on metal. Glancing through the window she saw Trevor's car turning into the drive.

"Paul, Charlie. Daddy's back with James!"

The pirates were left stranded on a tropical beach as the boys rushed into the hall and out through the front door, followed only slightly more sedately by their mother. As the car drew to a halt the boys jumped up and down excitedly, waving through the car window at James who managed a big smile but didn't wave back.

Kate opened the rear passenger door and touched James gently on the forehead.

"Welcome home, brave boy. Trevor, can he get out himself? I don't want to hurt him."

"What do you think, can you get out OK?" Trevor turned to look teasingly at James.

"Course I can!" And to demonstrate, James turned slowly on his seat and edged to the door, sliding along until his feet hung outside. He paused a moment before lowering himself gently to the ground with a grin of triumph.

Charlie and Paul held back now, overawed by their brother's evident fragility. However, their awe quickly changed to laughter.

"You're wearing Daddy's shirt!"

"It's huge! And where's your arm?"

"Underneath." James used his free hand to show that his left arm was in a sling and the shirt was just draped over it.

"Is Daddy wearing your shirt? Bet he looks silly too!" Paul found this hilarious.

Not looking at Trevor, Kate planted a careful kiss on James's cheek. "Well done, darling. We're thrilled you could come home so soon. Let's go inside for supper and you can tell us what it was like in hospital."

"Penne Bolognese then plums and ice cream," chirruped Paul, grinning as they followed Kate and James into the hall.

Trevor was left to get out of the car unobserved. As he joined them in the hall another round of laughter erupted.

"You're not wearing a shirt at all!" Paul hooted, and poked his father in the ribs.

Kate turned round and saw that indeed, Trevor was wearing a jacket over his bare torso.

"We didn't think to take something easy for him to come home in. There's no way he could get into his T-shirt, and it was dirty anyway, and a bit torn. I threw it away in the hospital. My shirt was the only option. I felt pretty silly walking to the car." In a gesture meant to amuse Kate, he pulled the jacket back and thrust out his bare chest, Tarzan fashion.

Unable to be natural with him Kate didn't respond but continued towards the kitchen. Trevor turned away letting his jacket fall closed, the hurt visible in the droop of his shoulders.

"Now you two, please be careful with James. The sling you can see but his cracked ribs you can't and they're probably very painful." She looked sideways at James who nodded. "So, no rough games. James, do you feel up to staying up for supper or would you like to lie down upstairs?"

"I'm very hungry. Is it long till supper?"

No, maybe fifteen minutes or so, I've just got to cook the pasta. How about watching a bit of the pirate film Charlie and Paul were watching? You could lie on the sofa."

James nodded acquiescence. "But I think I'd rather sit up."

The older boys resumed their positions and Kate arranged cushions to make James comfortable before handing the remote to Charlie. The pirates came to life and Kate retreated to the kitchen, setting to work on the final preparations. She stiffened as Trevor came in and hovered by the door.

"Anything I can do?" His voice was unusually tentative.

"No." But then, "Oh, yes, you can grate some cheese."

Grateful for constructive activity, Trevor took the Parmesan from the fridge, armed himself with the grater and a plate and set to work on the end of the counter furthest from Kate, not trusting himself to speak.

Kate drained the pasta, gave the sauce a final stir then disappeared to fetch the boys.

"Sit down, everyone," she said brightly. "Do you need any help, a cushion, James?"

"I'll get one." Paul jumped up, returning with a cushion from the sofa and Kate helped James settle onto his chair.

Ignoring Trevor, Kate served everyone in silence. The boys sensed the tension and were quiet too.

Taking a deep breath and turning to James, Kate said, still in her unnaturally bright voice, "I've arranged for you and me to stay with Granny and Grandpa for a few days. We'll go first thing after breakfast tomorrow."

"You what?" Trevor looked up from his plate and slammed his fork down, spattering sauce on the table. "What the fuck is going on with you, Kate?" His voice was unpleasantly loud and the boys looked at him in astonishment.

Kate fixed her eyes on him with such a stare that he flinched and hung his head.

"We'll talk when the boys are in bed." Kate hid her nervousness behind a reassuring smile at the boys who were looking wonderingly from one parent to the other. Charlie and Paul exchanged looks. Such an outburst was almost unheard of.

Trevor got up abruptly and left the room.

Chapter 19

The shocked silence was broken by gentle sobbing from James. Kate reached out to put her arm around him but as she gathered him to her, he screamed in pain.

"Oh, my darling, I forgot for a moment. I'm so sorry. Oh dear. Look, hold my hand and squeeze it tight." She held out her hand to James who took it hesitantly. "Now squeeze, really, really hard. It will help just a little bit."

James obeyed, the tears now streaming down his face.

"Is it my fault Daddy's so cross?" he said, hiccupping through the tears. "Because I ran into the road?"

"No, of course not, Jamie darling. But you gave us a terrible fright, we were really scared you might be badly hurt. I tried to sleep in the chair in your room last night but I was too worried to sleep properly. And I know Daddy had a bad night, too, so we are both exhausted and maybe that's why Daddy was so upset."

James nodded, only partially convinced.

Paul spoke up, looking to Kate for support. "Charlie and I should have stopped you, so it's partly our fault too."

"Yes, we're really sorry," said Charlie. "Honestly, it all happened so quickly, we didn't have time to think."

"Let's not blame anyone," said Kate hastily. "I'll talk to Daddy later and calm him down. Your food is probably a bit cold now; shall I put it in the microwave, or shall we go straight to pud?"

The answer was obvious from their faces.

"Charlie, please get the ice cream out. Paul, get the bowls."

James stopped crying and held out the bowl Paul handed him. "Lots, please."

Kate kept up cheerful chatter as they ate, James's appetite clearly whetted by his abstemious day in hospital. "Now, it's a bit early for bed for you two," looking at Charlie and Paul. "Why don't you finish the pirate film while I help James get ready for bed."

"Must I go to bed already? I'm not tired yet."

"Well, maybe watch a bit of the film while I clear up – but no complaints when I say stop!"

All three boys disappeared into the sitting room. Kate heard a brief squabble over who should work the remote, but it was soon replaced by laughter and comments on the pirates' antics. She cleared the table and loaded the dishwasher before joining the boys. She let them watch for a few minutes before tapping James lightly on his good shoulder.

"Come on now. Bedtime. It's going to take longer than usual. A bath would be soothing; do you think you could manage that, or I could put a stool in the shower for you to sit on and let the hot water run down your back?"

James said the shower sounded fun so Kate fetched a plastic stool from the laundry room and, holding hands, they went upstairs. They hadn't bothered to take off Trevor's shirt before supper, so getting undressed was easy. Kate let the shower run to set a comfortable temperature, placed the stool strategically, unwrapped the bandage and helped James to sit so that the water warmed his back.

"Is that OK, not too hot, not too hard?"

"No, it's nice, I like it! It tickles a bit, but it doesn't hurt."

Kate took her shoes and top off, soaped a flannel and stepped into the shower to give James a gentle wash. She let him sit there for a few minutes longer before turning off the water and holding out a big fluffy towel, warm from the radiator. Wrapping him cosily, she dried him all over and re-wrapped the bandage. Pulling the pyjama top on was too painful so Kate fetched a soft shawl from her room and draped it round his shoulders before putting her top on again.

"There we go. Bed now. Would you like me to read your story, or shall I call Daddy?" she asked tentatively as they went into his room.

She wasn't altogether surprised when he said, "You, please."

"OK, hop in – look there's Freddy Teddy already in bed waiting for you!"

James clambered into bed and Kate made sure the sheet was loose. "How does that feel?"

"It's OK," but he flinched as he turned over.

"Maybe you'd be more comfortable propped up a bit. I'll get more pillows and some painkillers." Kate left to get the pillows and pills. Passing the sitting room, she saw that Trevor had joined the boys.

"James is in bed. I've come down for the painkillers. Where are they?"

"Still in the car. I'll get them for you." He got up and went out, returning a few moments later with the box of pills.

"I'm going to read James a story. Send Charlie and Paul up to bed in about half an hour. They can share a bath or have showers then you can read to them or they can have half an hour quiet time." Kate returned upstairs without waiting for an answer.

"So, here you are, two pills and a glass of water. Ready, steady, swallow!"

James obediently and expertly swallowed the pills.

"Well done! Very professional." Kate laughed and took the glass from him. "Now, which book would you like?"

"Winnie the Pooh. The one about the Heffalump, please." Then, plaintively, "Do I have to go to Granny and Grandpa's? I'd rather be with Charlie and Paul."

"They'll be at school all day so you couldn't play with them. Granny has already laid in special treats for you, Grandpa is planning games – and the dogs will be so pleased to see you."

James seemed satisfied. Kate sat carefully on the end of the bed, happy to read what had been one of her childhood favourites. She made the animals come alive but although James was totally absorbed, it was not long before he began to nod. Kate softened her tone until she was sure he was fully asleep.

Getting up carefully, she began to put together the few clothes and shoes he would need for the few days with her parents – she hoped it would only be a few days, and not drag on; a resolution was vital, though she couldn't think yet what it might be. Moving to her and Trevor's room, she selected some for herself and put them, with James's things and her wash bag, in a suitcase which she stowed in the spare room.

Feeling strangely guilty but determined going away was the right thing to do, she went downstairs where she found Trevor chivvying the boys to go up to bed.

"Come on, you two, if you don't hurry you'll have no time for reading." Trevor pretended to chase them.

"I'll come and say good night when you're in bed." Kate went to the laundry room and picked up the grassy underpants, rolling them into a ball and taking them into the kitchen where she finished tidying and laid breakfast.

When she heard Trevor coming down again, she went up, passing him on the stairs without comment except to say, "I'll be down in a few minutes and we can talk in the sitting room."

The boys settled with their books, she returned downstairs, collected the underpants and went into the sitting room where Trevor was sitting in one of the armchairs beside the fireplace. Was it habit or a token of appeasement that he had prepared the cafetière and cups set neatly on a tray with chocolate biscuits on a small plate? In a repeat of their first showdown, she sat in the opposite chair. She put the pants on her lap.

Chapter 20

Trevor looked up as Kate settled in her chair. He was wary, regretting his outburst in the kitchen. His confusion and resentment at Kate's behaviour since he arrived home had compounded the shock of her anger and violent slap in the hospital.

They sat for a moment in silence before Trevor stood and, with the raise of an eyebrow, offered Kate a cup of coffee.

"Would you like a biscuit with it?"

She nodded her acquiescence. He poured two cups and set a biscuit on the side of her saucer and two on his. He had barely eaten all day, just a sandwich from the hospital cafeteria, and his outburst had cost him most of his supper.

As Kate still said nothing, Trevor felt obliged to begin.

"I'm sorry about my rudeness. Putting it a bit more politely, what's going on, Kate?" He looked at her hopefully. "Why are you being so cold, so dismissive? It really hurts and I just don't understand."

At last Kate looked him in the eye.

"Do you really not understand how it felt to ring you at the London office only to be told you had left early for a parents' meeting when I knew perfectly well that there wasn't one? When you had told me you would be working late? When I knew you had had an affair with Nicola? When you were spending so much time in London? What did you expect me to think?"

Trevor lowered his head in acknowledgement.

"But I'm not having an affair, I promise. There's no-one else, honestly."

"Why should I believe you when you've lied so many times?"

"I'm not lying now." Trevor's voice rose. "For heaven's sake, Kate, look at me. I – am – not – lying." He spaced the words out for emphasis.

Kate carried on as if he hadn't spoken. "And then you tell me it's partly my fault. Talk about insult to injury."

Kate picked up the rolled ball of underpants and held them out to him.

"Tell me, how does a man get grass in his underpants?"

Trevor was totally nonplussed, his mind a blank. Exhaustion, guilt, confusion and misery combined to render him silent.

Kate stood up.

"If you can't answer that, what hope is there for us?" She went to the door. Turning, she faced him again. "I'm sleeping in the spare room tonight. I'll leave with James straight after breakfast." She left the room, only to return a second later.

"How could you do this to our lovely family? You've ruined everything." Then she was gone.

Trevor sat there, numb, coffee and biscuits forgotten. He was not surprised to find that tears were rolling down his cheeks. He didn't brush them away but stared unseeingly at the underpants. Suddenly, his mind clicked into gear. Underpants – police, search, smell of newly mown grass. His head jerked up; he began to stand and opened his mouth to call out to Kate but shut it again, realising that he had still not told her about his obsessive visits to Wimbledon. Cursing himself for his cowardice, he sat down again.

How, how on earth was he going to mend this awful situation? He couldn't imagine Kate listening now when they were both so distraught. Over breakfast? No, of course not with all the boys there. Maybe take Charlie and Paul to Kate's parents and explain there? No, that would be too embarrassing – and anyway, maybe she hadn't told her parents the whole story. He sat there, lowering his head to his hands, hoping for inspiration. None came.

For the second night running, he fell asleep where he sat, only waking when his head fell sideways and hit the arm of the chair. Looking at his watch, he saw it was already nearly midnight. Dragging himself to his feet, he lumbered to the stairs and hauled himself up clinging to the banister rail. Reaching their empty bedroom, he thought about knocking on the spare room door but realised he was in no fit state to deliver a coherent – and loving – explanation. Sighing, he undressed, dropping the clothes where they fell, made a quick visit to the bathroom then got into bed, pulling the duvet right up to his neck.

Sleep was more elusive this time, his racing mind causing him to toss and turn with each dead-end thought; he couldn't imagine how to broach his secret. Finally, exhaustion took over and he did sleep, woken bleary-eyed by Paul bouncing on the bed.

"Come on, Dad. Breakfast is ready and Mummy and James will be leaving."

Groaning, Trevor swung his legs over the side and sat up. "OK, I must have a quick shower then I'll come straight down. Go and tell the others I won't be a minute."

Paul left and Trevor stood under a stream of cold water, towelled himself vigorously, slipped on his dressing gown and made his way downstairs, knotting the cord as he went, unsure what he was going to say when he got to the kitchen.

The scene as he entered looked so normal, it was almost a shock. He made an effort to sound cheerful. "Morning, boys. How did you sleep, James? Shoulder not too painful, I hope?"

James smiled a little wanly. "It was OK," he said bravely.

Charlie was busy with his bowl of cereal, just looking up briefly in acknowledgement. Trevor was not surprised that Kate remained silent, avoiding his eye. He sat down and helped himself to cereal and coffee, horribly aware of how quiet the meal was compared with a normal school morning.

"Who's taking you to school this morning?" He looked at the older two.

"I think you are", said Charlie. "Mum's taking James to Granny's."

Kate nodded.

"OK, then make sure you've got everything and I'll take you, and come back to say goodbye to James and Mummy before I go to the office. I'll call Virginia to say I'll be in late but only stay a couple of hours."

The meal continued in near silence until it was time to leave for school. Trevor dressed quickly, collected the car keys and the older boys, kissed James on the head but studiously avoided Kate's eye. She made no attempt to speak to him but kissed Charlie and Paul. "Be good, I'll see you soon. Love you both."

The trio were almost at the car when Kate suddenly remembered the geranium. Grabbing the jar, she ran to the front door and was just in time to give it to Paul. "See," she laughed. "You nearly went without it. So much for remembering!"

"Thanks, Mummy." Paul clambered into the car clutching the jar, the geranium's scarlet petals just as bright as the day before.

Kate waved them off.

At school, Trevor parked and took the boys into the playground. He looked around for the member of staff on duty. "Hi, James won't be coming in for a few days. The damage wasn't as bad as we had feared, thankfully, but he needs rest."

"So pleased to hear it, Mr Martin. Do tell him we shall miss him – he's a lovely boy."

Trevor returned to the car and drove home, anxiety uppermost. How was he going to say goodbye to Kate? He turned into the drive and was shocked and saddened – but if truth be told, a little relieved – to see that Kate's car had already gone.

He was alone with his thoughts.

Chapter 21

Trevor opened the car door but sat for a moment before getting out and slamming it shut, hard.

"Why the fuck won't she believe me?" he almost cried, addressing the house, before leaning against the bonnet as the reality of the situation and his own cowardly stupidity hit him hard yet again. For the first time, he forced himself to face the worst outcome, the end of the life and family he loved so much. He ran his eye over the handsome grey stone house. "Not much equity to share there," he muttered, unaware that he was echoing Kate's words after their visit to the counsellor a year ago.

Pushing himself upright, he opened the front door and went in. The house felt different, abandoned, chilled, in spite of the sunny day. Instinctively he went to the kitchen but the sight of the uncleared breakfast table was too much. He retreated to the sitting room and slumped into the same chair he had slept in.

His thoughts were in such turmoil he gave up trying to think constructively but sat staring out of the window. His eye fell on the roses and for a moment he calmed; his inherited love of gardening, a passion also shared with Kate's parents, came to the surface as he admired the fullness of the blooms. Then he remembered that Kate had placed a bowl of roses on the ill-fated supper table. Was that a message? Hope?

The strident ring of the landline caused him to come back to the present with a start. Picking up the sitting room extension, he pulled himself together.

"Hello, Trevor Martin."

"Good morning. Are you coming to the office today? I've had a couple of calls you might want to deal with."

"Oh, hello, Virginia. Sorry, I meant to ring you earlier to say I'd be coming in late but we're a bit distracted here as you can imagine."

"Yes, of course. How is James?"

"Better than we had dared hope. Kate has just taken him to her parents for a couple of days' peace and quiet. Who rang?"

"One was Fred Crichton about the date for the management meeting. The other was Horst from Germany, said he had some interesting news. He didn't say what about but said you should call him."

Trevor groaned inwardly. There was no reason Horst should be calling except for his prurient interest in the Nicola affair. "Did he leave a number?"

"No, he said you had it. Are you coming in? I can manage here OK if not – just tell me what you'd like me to say to Mr Crichton. Nothing else urgent has come up."

"Thanks, Virginia, you're a star. I honestly don't feel up to coming in after two bad nights. Please tell Fred I'll discuss dates with him next week. Have a good weekend."

"Thanks, Trevor, you too." And she hung up.

Trevor sat down again, head in hands. Damn Horst. Damn, damn, damn. He knew he shouldn't call him – but just supposing he had found where Nicola was living. "No," Trevor said out loud. "I really don't want to know – no, not true, I mustn't know. Look where this bloody obsession with my son has got me."

Deciding he must put a stop to Horst's interest once and for all, he reached for his mobile to ring him, only to discover he'd sent a text.

Sorry missed you. Big news heard on grapevine. Nicola's husband's got a job with Staffords. In Bristol!

Trevor's heart sank to his boots. He felt cursed, haunted by that stupid affair and its consequences. The nightmare had to stop. Talking out loud again, he stood and addressed his reflection in the mirror over the mantelpiece.

"I, Trevor Martin, hereby promise I will tell Kate everything – everything." Then, taking a deep breath, continued. "Also, I will not try to find my son." Feeling better, but not sure how easy it would be now to keep the second promise, he looked at his watch and saw it was ten, still a bit soon to call Kate. Feeling energised by his resolution, he returned to the kitchen and set about tidying things away and loading the dishwasher.

10.30. He picked up the landline and dialled the Adamson's house rather than Kate's mobile, postponing the conversation with her for a few more minutes.

"Hello, Elizabeth Adamson."

"Hello, Elizabeth, it's Trevor. How are you? Has Kate arrived yet?"

"Fine, thanks. They got here about half an hour ago. She's out just now taking James for a short walk to refresh him after the journey. Shall I get her to call you?"

"Yes, please, on the landline. I'm not going in to work today – got to be around for Charlie and Paul. How did James cope with the journey?"

"Very well, considering."

Trevor managed a few more minutes of small talk before hanging up. The conversation reminded him that he did indeed have to look after the boys, to feed and entertain them over the weekend, and he needed to think ahead. Be practical, he said to himself. Tea, supper, breakfast. Checking the fridge and larder for staples, he was relieved to find they were well stocked, but he would have to buy fresh food for supper and maybe a cake as a treat at teatime. He was just making a shopping list when the landline rang. Heart pounding, he answered it immediately.

"Kate, darling, we must talk!"

"No, Trevor, it's Ann!" She laughed. "I just rang to talk to Kate and see how things were with James."

"Oh, sorry." Trevor was glad Ann couldn't see his embarrassment. He thought quickly. "We've got something important to decide and I'd left a message for her to ring me. I'm holding the fort here as she's taken James to her parents for a few days."

"Really? Why?" Ann affected surprise.

"She thought Charlie and Paul might be a bit too rumbustious with him."

"Well, tell her I called and she can ring me on my mobile. Do let me know if there's anything I can do to help. We're busy tomorrow but the boys could come and play with ours on Sunday, perhaps."

"Thanks, that's very kind. I'll call you." Trevor didn't prolong the conversation in case Kate rang.

He found it hard to settle to anything as he waited, thoughts on how to explain to Kate running through his head. After about an hour he rang her mobile but it was switched off so he rang the Adamsons again. It was Kate's father who answered this time. Trevor didn't bother with pleasantries:

"Hello Geoffrey, it's Trevor. Is Kate around now?"

"I'm not sure where she is. Hold on and I'll see if I can find her. A relief to see James is coping so well."

"Thanks."

There was a long pause before Mr Adamson returned to the phone. "I'm sorry, Elizabeth says Kate's having a rest and doesn't want to be disturbed. I'll ask her to call later. Give my love to Charlie and Paul – hope to see them soon."

Frustrated – and suspecting that Kate was deliberately avoiding him – Trevor decided to risk missing her and do the shopping before the boys needed fetching from school. The trip to their local Sainsbury's didn't take long and he was home within an hour. He immediately checked the phone for messages, his heart lifting when there was one, but it turned out to be a wrong number. Deflated, he unpacked the shopping and made himself a cup of coffee.

Reading the news on his iPad absorbed half an hour. Still no call. Deciding he needed to be active, he tucked his mobile safely into his pocket and went into the garden. Collecting gloves and secateurs, he set about dead-heading the roses and the flowers in the herbaceous border.

The silence from his phone was deafening.

Having done all the pruning that was necessary, plus some that wasn't, he looked at his watch again. 1.30. Lunch would take his mind off the waiting, he thought, and returned to the kitchen to eat some bread and cheese.

How much longer before he could call again? It would be humiliating to be told yet again by her parents that Kate wasn't available; they must be getting suspicious. What had she told them?

He went to his usual chair in the sitting room, leant back and closed his eyes. Sleep took over and it was with horror that, opening his eyes, he saw he was already late to collect the boys from school. Rather than take the time to walk as Kate often did, he rushed to the car and drew up outside the school, hugely relieved to see Charlie and Paul just inside the gate, talking to one of the teachers.

Trevor didn't bother to obey the school parking rules – he parked as close as he could and leapt out. The boys saw him at once and came over.

"So sorry I'm late," he said as he hugged them tight. Turning to the teacher, he apologised profusely and she smiled her forgiveness.

"How's James?" Charlie asked as soon as they were on their way.

"He's OK. Mummy and he arrived safely and he's even been for a walk."

"Can we talk to him when we get home?" Paul asked hopefully.

Trevor swallowed as he assured Paul that of course he could, praying that Kate had not put a phone embargo on James as well. Remembering the geranium, he quickly changed the subject to ask whether the flower sharing class had gone well. Hearing about it and their day passed the short time to home.

"OK, boys, I bought you a treat for tea! Put your school bags away and come to the kitchen."

No urging was needed. Trevor produced the chocolate cake with a flourish and poured glasses of milk before allowing himself to check his phone.

No messages.

Chapter 22

"Got any homework?" Trevor asked as the boys quaffed their milk and tucked into the cake.

"No, silly, it's weekend. We never have anything at weekends."

"We're too young!" piped up Paul, who had clearly been listening to adult discussion on homework overload at primary school.

Trevor laughed and ruffled Paul's hair. "Let me see if Mummy's mobile is on, then you can talk to James before he goes to bed." He dialled, letting it ring for quite a while before giving up. His frustration was now beginning to turn to anger. "I'll ring Granny. She'll get Mummy to call."

"Elizabeth Adamson."

"Hi, Trevor again. Charlie and Paul are very keen to talk to James, but Kate's not answering. Please could you ask her to call us before James goes to bed."

"Of course. Let me say hello to the boys before you hang up."

Trevor passed the phone to Charlie and turned on the speaker. Paul stood close.

"Hello, you two. Is Daddy looking after you properly?"

"Yes! He gave us chocolate cake for tea – the one with sugary creamy stuff on top. It was double yummy. Did you get any of those special chocolate biscuits that James loves?"

"We like them too," interjected Paul. "Will you get some for us when we come?"

"Of course, darlings." Mrs Adamson laughed. "You know Grandpa and I love spoiling you. Come and see us soon. Bye – no, here comes James!"

Suddenly presented with James, the boys fell silent, tongue-tied, not sure how to open the conversation. Trevor helped them out by asking if he was having a good time.

"Yes. There's lots to eat and the dogs are fun."

"Do they lick you a lot?" asked Paul. "Do they hurt your shoulder?"

"No. Mummy makes sure they don't jump on me indoors, and they're too excited chasing around when we go for walks with them. They're very funny when they think they smell something interesting."

"Wish we were there too. Can we talk to Mummy?" Charlie asked a little plaintively, not sure what else to say to James.

"She's in the bath 'cos she got all muddy when she fell over." James giggled. "It was very funny. She was trying to catch Tolly and slipped where Grandpa had been watering the vegetables and she fell on her face in the potatoes!"

They all joined in the hearty laughter and Trevor felt just slightly better that there was a good reason why Kate hadn't answered her phone.

Farewells were said, and the request repeated that Kate should ring later.

"Right, boys, why don't you get out of your school things and put your shirts in the wash. Then you can have an hour of TV or maybe play outside as it's such a lovely evening – no chasing balls into the road, though!" He smiled to make light of it. "I'm going to get your supper ready. Off you go."

Obediently the two disappeared and Trevor got to work, laying the table, preparing the lamb chops, potatoes and beans, an easy and popular supper. He decided to eat with them, relaxing as he worked, happy shouts from the garden punctuating his efforts as the boys set up the portable goal and took it in turns to be goalie.

"Supper time," he called through the kitchen window. "Come in and wash your hands."

The boys sniffed appreciatively as they entered the kitchen and took their places, hands duly washed. Trevor poured himself a glass of wine and they ate companionably. He hadn't thought about a dessert but produced the remains of the chocolate cake.

"Ice cream with it?" he asked with a smile. "Or is that a silly question?" Not waiting for an answer, he fetched it from the freezer and served them all.

"OK, all done. Please clear the table and put the plates in the dishwasher, then you've got an hour before bath time."

Left alone, Trevor washed up the cooking pans then paused, looking vacantly out of the window. He saw the boys had left the goal on the lawn but he didn't bother to go out to put it away. In fact, he felt he couldn't be bothered to do anything. The strain of keeping up a cheerful front was draining. After a few minutes he metaphorically shook himself into the present. He needed to keep busy to stop constantly anticipating Kate's phone call. He decided to join the boys. Leaving the kitchen, he could hear them playing upstairs.

He found them sprawled on the floor of their bedroom, the Snakes and Ladders board open between them.

"Any chance I could join in, or is it only for two? It's such a long time since I played it I can't remember."

"We've played it enough. Let's play something else with you. How about Battleships – or Monopoly?" said Charlie.

"They take rather a long time, don't they?" Trevor demurred. "But I've got an idea. Have you got any playing cards – oh, of course you have. Get them out and let's play Pelmanism – the memory game. It's ages since we last did, and it's fairer to play it without James."

Cards spread out face down, they took it in turns to find matching pairs. Trevor found the concentration good for keeping his mind occupied and half an hour passed quickly with honours even, though he had to make a deliberate error or two.

"Right, time to stop. Cards away and get ready for your bath. I'll get the water running."

While the boys bathed, Trevor inspected their room, putting dirty clothes in the wash basket and getting out their pyjamas. He crossed over to James's room and stood in the doorway, thinking how much worse the accident could have been, but also inevitably returning to the disaster of his conversation with Kate. He made himself return to the boys.

Dried, pyjama-ed and in bed, the boys were ready for their bedtime reading. Charlie picked up Harry Potter, but on impulse Trevor suggested he might read to them from a book he chose for a change. The boys agreed, intrigued, and Trevor went down to his study where he knew he had a book about Shackleton's voyage to the Antarctic. After explaining a bit of the background, he opened the book at the point where the boat became trapped in the ice.

The boys were riveted, the line drawings of the boat and the men bringing it to life. When Trevor stopped, saying it was time for sleep, they clamoured for more.

"Please, Daddy, we've got to know what happened," Paul pleaded. "Did they get it out OK?"

"Sorry, lads, that's enough for tonight. But if you're good, I'll read some more tomorrow."

Delighted to have made such a good choice, Trevor kissed them good night. "Lights out in half an hour or no more Antarctic tomorrow!"

Back downstairs, Trevor was faced with the rest of the evening alone with his thoughts. He switched on the TV but couldn't concentrate. As the telephone remained silent, his annoyance – no, anger – with Kate began to rise again. How could he fulfil his promise to tell her everything if she wouldn't speak to him? He stood and paced the room. No, he would not call again; it was her turn, he'd tried often enough.

For want of any other ideas, he went back to his study, picking over the papers on his desk, even playing a couple of games of patience on his computer. The continuing silence weighed on him and on impulse he pulled out a clean sheet of paper. Picking up the nearest pen, he began to write rapidly.

Dear Kate,

I'm sitting here waiting for you to call. I've been waiting all day and I'm frustrated, angry (yes, angry) and very unhappy. I made a solemn vow today to tell you everything in the hope that you will finally believe me, but how can I when you won't talk to me – and last time I tried to tell you, you said you wouldn't believe a word I said. However, I repeat, <u>I am not having an affair</u>.

This hurts, really hurts.

I love you. If you love me, you will listen and believe me.

Trevor

He felt better for writing so honestly, but reading it through, Trevor knew that he couldn't send it; it was too abrupt as well as being almost illegible, he had written so fast.

Although it was only 9.30, he decided he needed a good night's sleep. He switched off the lights and was about to go upstairs when he was suddenly struck by a possible way to bring Kate back home. Putting the study lights back on, he picked up the phone and dialled his parents.

"Hi, Mum, sorry to ring a bit late. Hope I'm not disturbing you."

"No, love, we were just watching telly, nothing special. Nice to hear you – you don't ring often enough." Although her tone was light, there was still a hint of complaint. "How's James, poor lad?"

"Sorry, Mum, I've been a bit distracted. James is doing remarkably well. Kate's taken him to her parents for a couple of days' peace and quiet. I'm on my own with Charlie and Paul for the weekend and I just wondered whether we might come to visit you tomorrow. They love coming to you, and I thought maybe we could combine it with a visit to the beach."

"Lovely idea!" She called out to her husband: "John, Trevor says can he come over with the boys tomorrow, then take them swimming. OK?"

Trevor heard his father's enthusiastic 'yes'.

"That's super." Trevor thought quickly. "How about we come over about 10.30? I'll bring their swimmers and towels."

"Perfect. I'll do something about some lunch – maybe even a picnic. Let me surprise you!"

"Thanks, Mum. Love to Dad, see you tomorrow – oh, by the way, I've a couple of errands to do. OK if I leave the boys with you for an hour or so?"

"Course it is. See you tomorrow. Bye."

Feeling better for having a plan, Trevor switched the lights off again and went to bed.

Chapter 23

Trevor looked at the clock as he woke – 7.30. The window was bright with morning sunshine. Feeling refreshed from the best night's sleep he'd had in days, he got up and opened the curtains. It was indeed a lovely morning, fresh but full of promise, perfect for fun with the boys. He opened the window and leant out; he could smell the grass and even a faint scent of roses.

He was impatient to get on with the day, implementing his plan to bring Kate home, ensuring the boys didn't have time to dwell on her and James's absence. Pulling on his dressing gown he went downstairs and set the coffee machine to work. He had just finished laying the table and was sitting down savouring his first cup when Paul appeared.

"That smells nice," ventured Paul.

"Want to try it?" Trevor motioned him closer and lifted the cup.

Paul's appreciatively wrinkled nose was buried in a grimace as he took a sip. "It's disgusting," he cried, running to the sink and holding his mouth under the running tap. "Yuk, how can you drink it?"

Trevor laughed sympathetically. "I was like you until I went to uni and my friends were drinking it. I didn't want to be left out so I made myself keep trying it until I got to like it too. Is Charlie awake?"

"Yes, he's reading."

"Why don't you pop up and tell him breakfast is ready and when you're both here I'll tell you what we're going to do today."

Paul disappeared, reappearing a few moments later with Charlie who seemed a bit subdued, giving Trevor a perfunctory kiss before sitting down and helping himself to Frosties. Paul was chattier.

"What are we doing today? Going to Granny's?" he asked between mouthfuls of cornflakes.

Charlie looked up sharply, then down again as Trevor set out his plan.

"No, we're going to Nana and Pop's as we haven't seen them for ages. Nana's making a picnic to take to the beach. It's such a lovely day, we'll be able to swim. As soon as you've finished breakfast, go up and get dressed and look out your swimmers."

"Goody! Let's take a football." Paul swallowed his last mouthful. "Pop always likes to play."

Paul left the kitchen but Charlie lingered. He looked at his father.

"Dad, why won't Mummy talk to us? Is something wrong? Is it James?"

Trevor stood and went to sit next to Charlie. Putting his arm around him and doing his best to sound reassuring, Trevor decided on a half-truth.

"I'm not really sure, but it may be because Mummy and I had an argument. We don't often argue so it was a bit hard. I think she's cross with me, but hopefully she'll get over it soon and things will get back to normal."

"What was it about?"

"It's complicated, too hard to explain now. Why don't you go and get ready. I've got to get dressed too – and get beach towels and the ball." Trevor gave his son a quick hug and moved away to forestall any more questions. He busied himself for a few moments, clearing the table and putting things away and was relieved when he heard Charlie's footsteps on the stairs.

Trevor returned to his room, dressed quickly in shorts and a T-shirt, found his trunks and three beach towels then went to check on the boys. He found them having a pillow fight, bedclothes all in a heap and neither boy dressed.

"Come on, you two, get a move on. Don't forget clean pants. And make your beds!" He grinned to soften his words but clapped his hands for emphasis. "Downstairs in ten minutes."

Leaving them to it, Trevor went down to the garage for the football and a holdall. Returning to the house, he packed his things into the bag and called up. "Ready?"

"Just coming!" Paul came clattering down, waving his swimming trunks like a flag. Charlie followed a little more sedately. Trevor could sense that his explanation over breakfast had not been entirely convincing, so he redoubled his efforts to be cheerful and appear unconcerned.

"Right," Trevor looked at his watch. "I told Nana we'd be there about 10.30 so we're in good time. Put your cozzies in the bag." He held it out for them and patted his pockets to be doubly sure he had his keys, phone and wallet. The three of them went out to Trevor's car. "Hop in while I just close the house." He turned back into the house and checked the windows were closed, before collecting his iPad from the study and emerging, locking the front door behind him.

In the car, he turned to look over his shoulder. "Strapped in?"

"Yes, Daddy," they replied in chorus, well used to this routine enquiry.

The drive down to the city centre went quickly. It was still early, so the Saturday shopping crowds were not yet in evidence and they were soon through the centre, up into the southern suburbs and out into the country.

"Now I don't have to concentrate so hard, how about playing the story game?" Trevor gave a questioning glance back in the mirror, hoping to keep their minds busy.

"OK. Can I start?" Paul was always keen to set the ball rolling. Not waiting for an answer, he began. "Once upon a time, a giant frog lived in that pond." He pointed out of the window.

"You next, Charlie," urged Trevor as the silence became a bit long.

"I haven't got any ideas. You go."

"OK. One day the giant frog got worried because it hadn't rained for ages and the pond was beginning to dry up. Over to you, Charlie."

"The frog thought for a minute, then remembered he had heard another frog croaking what sounded like an invitation."

"The giant frog, whose name was Warty, decided to try to find the other frog in case it lived in a better pond." Paul was ready with his line.

The game got well underway and the time passed quickly.

"Look, we're nearly there!" Trevor interrupted the flow. "Let's save the rest for the way home."

Sure enough, they were approaching the village where his parents lived and in no time Trevor pulled up in front of their cottage. The car had barely come to a halt when his mother appeared on the front path. The boys were unbuckled and out of the car before she reached the gate. Arms wide, she clasped them both to her.

"Hallo, you gorgeous creatures." She planted smacking kisses on their cheeks and ruffled their hair before pushing them away to arm's length. "My goodness, how you've grown!" She looked up at Trevor, who by now was standing behind them. "What a pair!" she laughed, giving him a hug and a kiss too. "But how's James?"

Trevor answered lightly. "Coming on well, nothing special to report."

"Come on in, Pop's waiting for you." She gave the boys a gentle push and urged them up the path, Trevor following on behind.

"John, they're here!"

Trevor's father emerged from the kitchen and added his hugs and kisses. "Great to see you, it's been a while."

"Yes, sorry about that, but we've got all day today to make up for it – at least, the boys have, but I've got an errand to do for an hour or so. Can you and Mum look after them until I get back and then we can go to the beach?"

"It would be a pleasure, wouldn't it, Susan?"

Trevor's mother laughed her agreement. "I'm sure we can keep them busy, no worries."

"Actually, I've got something to do and could use some help." Mr Martin turned to the boys. "You two any good with a saw and loppers? I cut a tree down yesterday and the small branches need chopping, then there's logs to stack."

Charlie and Paul's faces lit up as they followed their grandfather into the garden. Trevor laughed as he turned to his mother.

"That hit the spot! I'll get off right away and shouldn't be more than an hour or so." Trevor gave his mother a quick kiss and returned to the car.

It wasn't far back to the café he remembered noticing on the way. He parked, picked up his iPad and went inside, ordering a black coffee before sitting down. Opening the iPad, he connected to the internet and set his plan in motion. He soon found a florist near Kate's parents, took out his phone and dialled the number.

"If I order now, can you deliver this afternoon?" he asked, as soon as the shop answered.

"Yes, sir, if it's nearby."

"It is. Please can you send 14 red roses to Kate Martin at the following address." He gave the Adamsons' address. "And the note to go with it is: 'Please count the roses and read my email. All my love, Trevor'. Just read that back to me, could you, please."

The florist read it out correctly. Trevor thanked her profusely, paid and hung up. Part one of the plan done. Going back to his iPad, he opened his email and began to write.

The words didn't flow as easily as in his impassioned scrawl the night before, as he knew he had only one chance to get it right. After reading it through one last time, he put it in the 'drafts' folder, reckoning it would be best to send it later when the flowers were likely to have arrived. Looking at his watch, he was surprised to see it was nearly noon. Swallowing the last of his now cold coffee, he paid his bill, thanked the waitress and hurried out to the car.

Back at the cottage, he heard the boys in the back garden so went through the side gate to join them. As soon as they saw him, they rushed over and pulled him to the end of the garden.

"Look what we've been doing!" Paul pointed to a neat pile of logs and small branches. "Pop taught us how to use the saw and loppers, and Charlie even got to chop some logs! Then we had a wheelbarrow race."

Trevor looked up questioningly at his father who nodded. "They've been a great help and it was fun, wasn't it, boys?"

They both nodded enthusiastic agreement. Charlie bent his right arm and clenched his fist. "Feel my muscle," he commanded his father who obliged, laughing.

"Very impressive, well done both of you. Now, if Nana's ready, I think we should set off. We'll take my car as it's a bit bigger."

It took very few minutes to load the car with the two picnic baskets his mother had prepared. Trevor motioned her to sit in the front with him, while his father sat in the back between the boys.

"OK, Burnham-on-Sea or Clevedon?" Trevor asked his parents as he turned on the engine.

"Oh, Burnham, it's a sandy beach." His mother didn't hesitate. In the mirror, Trevor saw his father nod in agreement.

It was only a short drive to the beach and Trevor knew it was highly unlikely the flowers would be delivered before four, so he was able to join in the fun wholeheartedly – swimming, eating, games of tag and football. The beach was busy, which added to the holiday atmosphere but as the afternoon progressed, Trevor's thoughts turned inevitably to Kate. Impatient to learn whether she had responded, at 3.30 he called a halt.

"I think we should be getting home soon," he said, to be met by a chorus of "not yet, another swim, please, just a bit longer." Laughing, he held his ground. "We've had lots of fun, and I think we've exhausted Nana and Pop and we should take them home." He glanced meaningfully at his parents to ensure their agreement.

The journey back to the cottage was still cheerful and, the remains of the picnic unloaded, there were cuddles and kisses and injunctions to come again soon.

"It's been lovely having you to ourselves today," Trevor's mother said as she hugged her son goodbye. "But do bring Kate next time, won't you."

Trevor nodded, his nervousness increasing by the minute. To keep his spirits up, he returned to the story of Warty the frog which, getting sillier and sillier with each added sentence, managed to fill the time until they were home.

The car unloaded, swimming things rinsed and hung up to dry, Trevor could bear it no longer. Settling Charlie and Paul with milk and biscuits in the kitchen, he took his iPad and phone into the study. His heart was heavy when he saw there was still nothing from Kate. He read his draft email once more, took a deep breath and pressed 'send'. Telling himself Kate would need time to read his message, and reply – and he sent up a fervent prayer that she would – he went back to the boys.

Chapter 24

On Saturday morning Kate was roused, not by boys bouncing on her bed, but by her mother setting a cup of tea on the bedside table.

"No hurry to get up, darling, James is downstairs with his grandfather. Enjoy a bit of peace!"

"That's lovely, Mummy, thanks. I'll be down in a while."

As she luxuriated in the unusual treat, Kate let her mind run through the past 24 hours, starting with the flight from home, her parents welcoming her and their grandson with gentle warmth and an irresistible offer:

"James, sweetheart, you must be hungry after the journey. Am I right you'd like a chocolate biscuit to keep you going until lunch?"

"Yes, please!"

Kate, smiling, had followed James as he happily accompanied his grandmother to the kitchen where they were joined by Tolly and Cobbold, the Golden Retrievers named after the beer favoured by her father when he had lived in Suffolk. The dogs had a second sense where biscuits were concerned. "Down, that's mine!" yelped James as he defended his treat.

"Coffee, darling?" Mrs Adamson had gestured to the kettle.

"Yes, please, then I'll take James for a short walk to wake us up after the drive."

Refreshments consumed, she and James had set off, returning to lunch then the proffered biscuit tin, prompting further remonstrations.

"Honestly, Mummy, you're spoiling him!" She'd conceded that James could have one biscuit, but then have a rest.

Downstairs, she had found her father about to go into the garden.

"Fancy a walk round the garden? The early potatoes are coming on a treat and your mother's delphiniums are terrific this year." Kate's father gave due credit. The vegetables were his passion.

The garden was looking wonderful and provided enough to talk about to avoid any awkward questions from her father, though it was her mother who was more likely to do any probing – not that Kate had, as yet, given her any cause for concern.

When James woke and came downstairs, he was allowed more biscuits.

"Mummy, you're shameless! James, if you keep eating biscuits like that, you'll get fat – and rot your teeth!"

Grandparental shoulders were shrugged. "If we can't spoil our youngest grandson now..."

"James, would you like to help me dig up some new potatoes for your supper?" Mr Adamson was good at making popular suggestions, but fortunately he must have remembered the ribs and shoulder as he'd added: "I'll dig and you choose which ones you want."

Bringing herself back to the present, Kate finished the cup of tea then stretched herself in the wide bed, almost wishing she hadn't accepted her father's invitation to join them – though a smile lurked at the corners of her mouth as she returned to the scene.

The three of them had set off for the vegetable garden, followed by Tolly and Cobbold. As they neared their goal, Tolly spotted a bird digging for worms among the potatoes and leapt forward. Not noticing that the earth was very wet where the sprinkler had been on, Kate had dived to stop him and fallen face down in the mud. James's shrieks of laughter were underscored by her father's guffaws. Deciding all dignity had already been forfeited, she had joined in, even rubbing a bit more mud onto her face for greater effect.

Leaving the potatoes for later, they had gone back to the house followed by the dogs who seemed subdued by the merriment.

"Granny, come and look at Mummy!" James called his grandmother. "She fell in the potatoes."

Mrs Adamson, too, had laughed at her mud-besmirched daughter, saying, as if Kate were still a child, "You'd better go and have a bath, sweetheart. Put those dirty things out and I'll pop them in the machine."

Her parents had taken charge of entertaining James and reading to him at bedtime, a task which Mr Adamson always tried to reserve for himself as he loved impersonating animals, baddies, fairies and any other characters. Kate remembered once hearing him roaring convincingly like a racing car, prompting her to imagine him acting it out as well – spinning an imaginary wheel and leaning as he took the corners too fast.

The adult evening had begun with a glass of wine on the patio, followed by a kitchen supper. Inevitably there were questions about the accident.

"What was he doing when it happened? How come he was in the front garden?" her father wanted to know.

"They were playing basketball using the hoop Trevor had put up on the garage and I was making tea for them. When I heard the screeching of the tyres and ran out, my heart was in my mouth. He really did look bad, sprawled in the road almost under the car – Paul even asked if he was dead. Luckily, the driver had called an ambulance and we got to the hospital very quickly. But sitting in the room with him – waiting, longing for him to wake up – was ghastly. In the end, we took it in turns to stay and it was Trevor who was with him when he did wake."

"Did they do scans and things?"

"Of course, and you can imagine our relief when we got the verdict that it was mild concussion and just a bruised shoulder and a couple of cracked ribs."

"I have to say I'm glad we didn't know about it until he was home," her mother had confessed.

"But what about you, how have you been keeping?" Kate had diverted the conversation to her parents' activities, the village, her sister in the US who had said she might visit again soon, and other family members.

She'd pleaded tiredness after a while. "It's nearly ten, would you mind if I went to bed now?" She felt genuinely weary enough to sleep well and not lie awake thinking about Trevor.

"Of course, darling. Sleep well."

Kate kissed both of them good night. "Thank you for taking us in – how lucky you had a free weekend. It's lovely to be here." She went upstairs and straight to bed, not bothering with another bath, just wanting oblivion.

******

Returning to the present and deciding she really should get up and have breakfast, Kate had a quick shower and went down to the kitchen. She was greeted by a happy James tucking into toast and marmite, and the energising smell of freshly brewed coffee.

Later, as Kate and her father were teaching James to play dominoes, the two dogs asleep at their feet, Mrs Adamson came into the sitting room waving a newspaper excitedly.

"Look what I've found in yesterday's local rag. There's a country fair today at Chesdon – sheep shearing, dog trials, pony rides, bouncy castle, children's petting farm, food stalls. It's not far from here. Would that be fun, James?"

James looked questioningly at his mother. "Can we go, please, Mummy? It sounds really good."

Kate looked doubtful. "I'm not sure you're up to it yet, it's only three days since the accident."

"Oh, pleeeease Mummy." His eyes twinkled knowingly. "I promise I won't ask to go on the bouncy castle!"

Kate's parents smiled indulgently and Kate could sense she was outnumbered. "Well, maybe..."

"I think it's a good idea. Support local activities, I say," Mr Adamson chimed in.

His wife's face fell. "Oh, dear, I've just thought of something. What about the dogs? We can't take them."

"I could stay with the dogs and you all go without me. I honestly wouldn't mind, as I'm still pretty tired from the last few days," Kate offered.

"Really? Are you sure?" Kate's mother looked doubtful. "What do you think, Geoffrey?"

"If Kate doesn't mind, I think it's a good solution. We don't often get a chance to have a grandson all to ourselves. Good chance to spoil him rotten, eh, James?" He ruffled his grandson's hair. "And you dogs won't know what you're missing." He chuckled as he tickled their ears.

"No, really, go and have fun. It will be something new for James." Kate smiled. "Just make sure you mind those ribs, darling, and ask Granny and Grandpa to bring you home if they hurt or you get tired."

James jumped up and kissed her. "Thanks, Mummy. I promise I'll be good."

"OK, that's settled." Mrs Adamson looked at her watch. "It's 10.30 now, let's try to leave in half an hour. Just finish your game, Geoffrey, and tidy up. Kate, will you be OK making something from the fridge for lunch? Come to the kitchen and I'll show you what there is."

Kate followed her mother, listening obediently as the contents of the large refrigerator were pointed out to her.

"There's plenty of fresh bread in the bin, too." Mrs Adamson paused. Appearing to busy herself checking the bread, she half turned to Kate. "Is everything all right at home, darling? You seem a bit distracted, a bit low. And I've noticed you haven't been taking Trevor's calls."

Kate swallowed before replying. "To tell you the truth, we did have a bit of a row. Not something we're used to, and it sort of escalated. I decided it would be a good idea to have a couple of days apart to cool down."

"Did Trevor agree?"

"I didn't ask him."

Mrs Adamson looked up sharply, worried by the bitterness in Kate's tone, but Kate had turned away and was leaving the kitchen. Sighing sadly, knowing that she was unlikely to get more information then, Mrs Adamson too left the kitchen and went to get ready for the fair.

When everyone had left, Kate decided to curl up on the sofa with a good book. She picked out a thriller, made herself a cup of coffee and returned to the living room, the dogs moving over to be near her.

Kate's protestations about tiredness were only too true, and the thriller was not sufficiently exciting to keep her from nodding off. She was roused by Tolly nuzzling her leg and was surprised to see it was already almost one o'clock.

"Need to go out, boys?" She led the way to the back door. She had clearly judged correctly as the dogs rushed out. Legs were cocked against trees at the end of the lawn before a pretend fight and a chase ending with them rolling over each other, tails wagging. Amused, Kate went back inside to prepare herself a sandwich, leaving the door open for their return.

Sandwich and an apple eaten, and another cup of coffee downed, Kate decided a long walk would do both her and the dogs good. "Time for walkies," she told them as she fetched their leads. "Let's go to the village the long way round."

It was a pleasant walk, nearly an hour by the back lanes which delivered them to the far side of the village. Kate walked slowly along the main street, admiring the old houses, perusing the shop windows, saying hello to one or two people she knew or who recognised the dogs. The pub was busy with families sitting in the garden enjoying the afternoon sun.

The road back to the house passed the grey stone church with its well-tended grounds. The yew trees were huge, the graves neat – some with fresh flowers, some with moss-covered stones. Kate stopped at the lych gate, suddenly struck with memories of her wedding there. Seeing the church doors were open, she tied the dogs to a boot scraper, told them to be good and that she wouldn't be long, and went in. There was a warm smell of polish and of fresh flowers from the vases filled with big white lilies in full bloom. The sun was strong through the stained glass windows, casting coloured patterns on the uneven stone floor. Kate stood in the doorway, breathing in the calm atmosphere and remembering. How happy she had been, how in love with Trevor, how right the whole world had seemed to her that day. And now... She gritted her teeth, refusing to cry.

Turning on her heel she left, her mind awhirl with memories and fears, anger and, lingering underneath, just a glimmer of hope that perhaps – just maybe – they could somehow salvage the situation. But the anger and fear were uppermost.

The dogs jumped up gleefully as she emerged. Untying them, she told them it was home time and they pulled her towards the gate. It was already four o'clock as she neared the house, wondering if her parents and James were back already. Their car was indeed in the drive, but a white van with writing on the side was just pulling out, too far away for her to read.

Once in the drive, she let the dogs off their leads. They raced round to the back garden, Kate following more sedately.

She was greeted at the back door by her mother who wore a big smile.

"There's been a delivery for you. It's in the sitting room."

Raising a surprised eyebrow, Kate went through the kitchen, on the way almost falling over James who grabbed her hand. "Come and look, Mummy." He didn't stop to tell her about his day out but pulled her through to the sitting room where her father stood holding a big bunch of red roses, beautifully wrapped and tied with a wide red ribbon.

"I think these are for you," he said grinning, holding them out.

Bemused, Kate took the roses, bent to smell them and saw there was an envelope inside. Taking it out, she opened it and read silently. 'Please count the roses and read my email. All my love, Trevor.'

Fighting to control her emotions, she laid the flowers on a side table and put the card in her pocket. She held James close to her. "They're from Daddy. Aren't they lovely."

Although her instinct was to run to her room, she held back. "How was your outing?"

James gabbled excitedly about what had clearly been a very successful day. On his mother's prompting, he hugged his grandparents with his good arm. "Thank you very much," he said formally, then giggled. "Wasn't it funny when the goat pulled the scarf off the little girl's mother and tried to eat it."

His grandparents agreed, laughing.

Kate interrupted the stories to say she was going to put the flowers in a vase, then to tidy up from her walk. She counted fourteen roses as she put them in water. Then, upstairs, she sat on her bed, took the card from her pocket and held it for a moment. A mixture of duty and curiosity made her reach for her phone and open it to email. Taking a deep breath, she started reading.

Dearest Kate,

I hate myself for causing you such unhappiness, for being too cowardly, too embarrassed, to tell you what prompted this stupid, stupid misunderstanding. I must start by reassuring you again that I am NOT having an affair. There is no woman but you in my life.

Yesterday I swore a solemn oath to myself to tell you the whole story, but you have refused to talk to me. I confess this hurts and I can only plead with you to come home and let me tell you everything, including about the greatest humiliation of my life which happened the afternoon of the accident.

I love you and I want to spend the rest of my life with you. If you will truly listen, I hope beyond hope that you will forgive me and help me.

If we can put this behind us and be the wonderful, happy family of just a few days ago, I hereby promise that every year, on the anniversary of the day you forgive my stupidity, I will give you a bouquet of roses, each year adding one more to the fourteen which celebrate our life together so far. Do we have enough vases for forty roses? Hopefully fifty or even sixty. If I can't afford fifty roses, then I will grow them for you in our garden.

I say again, I love you with all my heart, Kate Martin. Please come home tomorrow. I will cook a special dinner and then tell you everything.

All my love

Trevor

PS The boys keep asking about you and James. I've just told them we had an argument.

Conflicted but also moved – and intrigued by the reference to the humiliating experience – Kate read it through again. And a third time. Trevor's sincerity rang true. Could she refuse his plea? And there were the boys to consider.

She pressed 'reply'.

We'll come home tomorrow afternoon

Kate

Chapter 25

Subdued, but glad to have made the decision, Kate lingered in her room. Although touched by Trevor's email, she rationalised her decision to return home by thinking of Charlie and Paul and their need for her. After putting on some make-up to disguise any traces of her emotions, she returned to the sitting room. She noticed at once that her mother had put the roses in a prominent position by the window, where the afternoon sun falling on the blooms heightened them to an even richer red.

"Special occasion?" asked her father, apparently innocently, as Kate entered the room. "Anniversary or something?"

Mrs Adamson cast the briefest of glances at her daughter before interjecting quickly, "Honestly, Geoffrey, can't a man send his wife flowers from time to time without a special reason?" She looked pointedly at him.

Mr Adamson smiled and conceded defeat. Flowers and little gifts had never been his style, though he loved his wife dearly. "Sorry, love, I'll try to do better in future."

Blessing her mother for her tact, Kate returned the conversation to the day's outing.

"What else was good at the fair? I hope you didn't risk a pony ride!"

James seized the opportunity. "I wanted to, but Granny wouldn't let me – but there was a roundabout so I rode on a horse on that. Then we went to the animals and there was a big fat pig with lots of piglets. She was lying on her side and the piglets all lined up on her tummy to drink like this." He lay down carefully and moved his arm along his torso to demonstrate.

Tolly and Cobbold saw this as an invitation to play and had to be pulled off. Kate took the opportunity of the distraction to introduce her decision.

"By the way, I told Trevor we would come home tomorrow afternoon as I should be around to make sure everything's ready for school on Monday, and he said Charlie and Paul were asking when James would be back. I hope that's OK."

"Of course it is, darling. Whatever suits you." Kate's mother, relieved by the news, made no comment but reverted to the fair as a safe topic of conversation. "James, have you told Mummy about Grandpa and the coconut?"

"Grandpa said he used to go to fairs when he was a boy and always went to the coconut shy and there was one at the fair, so I made him have a go and he knocked the coconut off first time. I wanted him to do another one but the man in charge didn't look very pleased, said only one go but he did give us the coconut and Grandpa's going to cut it open for me to taste."

The fun of coconut tasting, more games and then supper helped the rest of the day pass quickly. Once James was in bed, the adults watched an old Charlie Chaplin film which Mr Adamson had recorded.

"Bedtime for me, I think." Kate stood up, yawning. "Good night. See you in the morning." She stooped to give each parent a kiss as she left the room.

Kate hoped that a long hot bath would calm her racing mind enough for her to sleep, but in bed she still found herself going over and over how she would behave with Trevor. Should she be cold and distant? Greet him with a hug or a kiss? Thank him for his email and the flowers? Ignore him and concentrate on the children? Finally, she dropped off, still undecided.

Sunday morning promised another fine day. Kate helped James get dressed. "What would you like to do this morning? We don't have to leave until after lunch."

James had no suggestions except, "Can we have more coconut?"

Over breakfast, Kate's father reminded her that he and her mother liked to go to church. "It's part of belonging to the village," he explained when she looked surprised. "We see everyone there – it's a good way of keeping up with the gossip since we don't go to the pub. Do you think James would like to come? Has he ever been to a Sunday service?"

After her visit to the church the day before, this didn't appeal to Kate at all. "No, we don't go to church and I'm not sure he would be happy to sit so long. He doesn't know the hymns either and can't read very fluently yet. Perhaps when he's a bit older."

"Maybe we can miss it this weekend – we don't see you that often, so it would be a shame not to have the morning together before you go home." He paused, then continued. "How about an excursion to the castle at Morvington? It's quite atmospheric and we can tell stories about Roundheads and Cavaliers and things."

"Brilliant idea." Kate smiled her agreement. "I'm sure James would love it – we haven't visited any castles for ages."

It was indeed a good expedition and they returned happy and energised from tramping over the castle in the sunshine. Lunch was followed by hugs and admonitions to come again soon en famille. Kate promised they would, crossing her fingers that they would still *be* a family after the coming showdown.

As she and James were getting into the car to leave, James suddenly stopped. "The flowers. We haven't got the flowers!"

Kate wasn't sure whether her subconscious had decided to leave them behind, or she had just plain forgotten but knew that now she would have to take them.

Mrs Adamson disappeared into the house, re-emerging a few minutes later with the roses wrapped in a black bin bag. "Not as pretty as when they arrived, but I've wrapped the stems in wet newspaper so they should be OK."

"Thanks, Mummy." Kate took the bag and stowed it flat on the floor of the car. "We'll have the air con on so they won't get too hot."

Final kisses exchanged and James strapped carefully into the back seat, Kate drove off, leaving her parents waving from the front door.

The drive back to Bristol was uneventful, the traffic light. It was just four o'clock when she left the motorway and arrived in the outskirts of the city. Pulling in to the side of the road, she stopped briefly. Reaching to the back seat, she stroked the sleeping James lightly on the knee. "Wake up, darling, we're nearly home."

James rubbed his eyes, still a bit sleepy, but then took in that he would soon see his father and brothers and tell them of his adventures. "Must tell Charlie and Paul about the goat and Grandpa and the coconut." He wriggled impatiently in his seat.

Kate was less eager as she still wasn't sure how to behave; she just hoped she could take her lead from Trevor. She didn't have long to think, as within a few minutes she had turned into their street and into the drive. She had barely come to a halt before Charlie and Paul came barrelling out of the front door and up to the car. They opened James's door almost before Kate had switched off the engine.

Charlie leant over to undo James's seat belt and started to pull him out.

"Ouch, that hurt!" shrieked James. "I can get out myself."

"Careful, careful!" Kate admonished them and, distracted, didn't notice Trevor emerging from the front door. Stepping out of the car, she turned and saw him. In spite of the anger which was still near the surface, her heart turned over at the look in his eyes – so tentative, so shy, so longing. She had to make herself hold back, though part of her wanted to hug and reassure him. Wait, wait until you hear what he has to say, said her head. She allowed him a tight smile.

"Let me get your bags," Trevor said, moving towards the car. "In the boot?"

Kate nodded and turned back to the car to lift out the roses. Feeling she couldn't remain silent, she held them out but avoided his eye. "They're beautiful. Thank you."

The boys had disappeared inside, so Kate locked the car and followed a silent Trevor into the house. "I must put them in water," she said, heading for the kitchen. Trevor followed her and she could feel his presence. She turned to him. "Look, I don't know how to behave with you now. Please can we put off talking until after dinner, just get on with normal things. You go and see James while I unpack." She kept all emotion out of her voice.

Trevor nodded. "I've missed him – so have Charlie and Paul. I'll go and see what they're up to." He paused. "But let me make you a cup of tea first. You could probably do with it after the drive."

Kate realised she was indeed thirsty. "Thanks. I'll have it when I've done the roses." She took the flowers into the laundry room where she kept the vases, found a large cut-glass one – a wedding present from his company, she remembered wryly – and arranged the flowers and took them to the sitting room.

Back in the kitchen, she found Trevor had set out tea things for two. He turned to her. "Let's sit down and plan for this evening. We've got to seem normal." He spoke firmly.

Kate was very aware that he had mastered his nervousness and taken control of the situation – a reversal of their roles at the previous showdown – and she didn't resent it; it made things easier.

"Good idea." She poured tea for both of them. "Why don't you spend some time with the boys while I get a snack ready for them. James will want to tell you about his weekend – he really did have fun." She couldn't help smiling. "If we're not careful, he'll want to go every weekend!"

“OK, I’ll finish getting their supper ready later – it’s mostly cooked already – and play a game or two with them after. At bedtime, I’ll read to James, if you read to Charlie and Paul. And while you do that and get dressed for a good dinner, I’ll start the cooking.”

His eyes actually twinkled, she noticed, but she wasn’t ready to be mollified yet and her voice turned cold. “OK, agreed. What time must I be ready?”

“Eight.” There was less twinkle now. “See you then.”

And that was the evening sorted, she thought, at least until the really hard bit.

Chapter 26

Kate was glad of practical things to do before the promised dinner. She had just finished unpacking and tidying up when the boys arrived, sent down by Trevor for a quick snack and drink.

"Any chocolate biscuits, Mummy?" James looked hopeful.

"No, it's too near supper – and anyway, you had far too many at Granny's." She turned to the other two. "You wouldn't believe how Granny spoilt James. Maybe I'll say we can't go again!"

This set off a chorus of protests.

"Not fair, we haven't had any."

"Mummy, you told them we would come again."

"I'll get the biscuit tin." This last one from Charlie, casting a resentful look at his mother.

"Quieten down! Charlie, put the tin back, sit and finish what I've put out, then Daddy will be ready to play a game or two with you before bed. I'm tired from the drive so I'm going to sit quietly for a bit. Daddy will read to you tonight, James, and I'm really looking forward to reading to you two for a change." She gave Charlie and Paul a quick hug each. "I missed you."

Trevor appeared as if prompted. "Football in the garden, or more games upstairs?"

"Football!" Paul didn't hesitate, but Charlie looked at his mother. "Is it OK for James?"

Kate, keen not to disappoint James who was clearly eager to play with his brothers, was quick to think of a solution. "I think James should be referee, make sure you play fair!"

Trevor found the football and took the three outside, leaving Kate to her own devices. She decided there was time for a shower. She could read to the boys in her dressing gown and get ready for dinner afterwards.

Pondering what to wear as she let the hot water run over her, she remembered that the last time they had had such an evening she had worn stockings and a suspender belt, but she knew she wasn't ready to seduce him this time – indeed, she had a feeling that, if Trevor was as convincing and romantic as his email, such a ruse would hardly be necessary. No! she told herself sharply. He's got a hell of an explanation to give to get through this. How on earth is he going to explain away his lies and the grass in his underpants. Her anger surfaced again.

She put on fresh underwear and wrapped her dressing gown round her, before drying her hair and laying out a pretty but not special flowery dress and matching sandals. Emerging from their room, she met Trevor.

"James is settled and ready for you to say good night. Charlie and Paul are in their room but haven't showered yet. I'm going down to finish getting dinner ready." He disappeared downstairs.

Kate found James curled up and clearly already sleepy. "Good night, darling. You've been really brave. Sleep well." She gave him a gentle kiss and whispered, "Love you, sweetheart," as she left the room. Again thinking of that dreadful evening a year ago, she gave silent thanks that Trevor seemed wholly recovered from his jealousy and anger at James not being his child. Until just a few days ago, she would have sworn that all was well with the Martin family. Suppressing these thoughts, she went to Charlie and Paul. She found them playing with Paul's fort.

"So, what did you two and Daddy do while we were at Granny and Grandpa's?" she asked as she sat on Charlie's bed. "Did you go out?"

Paul was quick to answer. “Yesterday we went to Nana and Pop’s and Charlie and I got to help Pop cut up a tree and we rode in his wheelbarrows then we all went to the beach and swam and had a picnic.”

“That sounds fun.” Kate was glad that Trevor had made the effort to do something special and to include his parents. She was aware that they didn’t see them as often as they perhaps should, given that Trevor was an only child and they lived not far away. She felt a little guilty that she had not encouraged more visits but, much as she respected what they had achieved from such a humble start, she could never find much to talk about with them apart from the garden and the children’s progress.

“But right now it’s time for showers and bed. You must be a bit sticky from football.”

Ablutions completed, the boys snuggled up either side of their mother for a Harry Potter story. Coming to a good stopping place, Kate put in a bookmark.

“That’s enough for now. Paul, you’re already half asleep – off you go into your own bed. Charlie, you can read for another ten minutes but please, please don’t make us come up again. Daddy and I are going to have a nice, quiet dinner and we absolutely don’t want to be interrupted.”

She tucked Paul into his bed and kissed him good night. Turning to his brother, she was struck by his slightly worried expression. “What is it, sweetheart?”

Charlie looked up at her pleadingly. “Please, be nice to Daddy.”

That arrow went straight to her heart. So, the tension had not gone unobserved.

“Don’t worry, darling,” she said, trying to sound casual. She stroked his cheek as she kissed him good night. “Remember, just ten minutes reading. Love you both, sleep well.”

Back in her bedroom, she dressed and then brushed her hair vigorously, almost punishingly so, before putting on some lipstick and eyeshadow. Might as well look good, she thought, but she drew the line at perfume – though she still had some, a gift from Trevor at Christmas.

It was almost eight as she made her way downstairs. The butterflies which always accompanied her at worrying moments were fluttering wildly as she entered the kitchen.

Trevor was stirring something in a pan, his back to her. The table was laid, complete with napkins, candles, and wine glasses. There were slices of chunky brown bread in a small basket, a fresh block of butter and a small bunch of flowers, blue ones, in the centre of the table. In each place were small bowls of tomato and feta salad topped with fragrant basil. There were other delicious aromas in the air as well.

"I did consider eating in the dining room, but I thought that was a bit over the top," Trevor said without turning round. "And anyway, this is easier. Hope you don't mind there's no tablecloth, but it seemed a bit artificial in the kitchen."

Kate managed a small laugh. "I agree on both counts. Is there anything I can do to help?"

"I don't think so – oh, yes, pepper and salt on the table, please. And why don't you pour us each a glass of white wine. There's a new bottle in the fridge."

Instructions obeyed, Kate approached Trevor's back, a glass in each hand. "Here's yours. Will you have it now?" she asked tentatively and was disconcerted as he turned round so close to her they were almost touching. For a second she thought he was going to kiss her. She shrank back defensively. Their eyes did meet, however, uncertainty clear in both, before they collected themselves and managed, "Cheers," before taking a sip.

"This is delicious," Kate pronounced unprompted. "We've not had this one before."

Trevor looked pleased that she'd noticed. "I went shopping for dinner this morning – Ann had invited the boys over to play – and the wine buyer was in the shop, so I asked his advice. We can always buy more. It wasn't that expensive," he added quickly and turned back to the stove. "I think we should have the starters now, as this is almost ready."

They sat down. Trevor passed Kate the bread. She took a slice and busied herself buttering it. Trevor did the same, and by silent agreement they started eating.

"This is very refreshing – lovely dressing," Kate said, licking some butter from her finger and wiping a drop of dressing from her chin.

"Thanks. I like something palate-cleansing to start with – sharpens the appetite."

Kate didn't respond; her appetite was definitely subdued by the circumstances and she hoped Trevor hadn't prepared anything too heavy.

"Finished?" Trevor held out his hand for her plate. "I need a couple of minutes for the next course. It's basically cooked, but I have to add in the bamboo shoots." He busied himself at the stove. "Could you get the warm plates out of the oven," he called over his shoulder. "Thanks."

The aromas Kate had noticed turned out to emanate from a chicken stir-fry, made colourful with slivers of red and yellow peppers and bright green baby beans. Trevor served them both, simultaneously asking, "Red wine or more white?"

"White, please – it really is good and will be nice with the chicken." She held out her glass which, to her surprise, was already empty. Nerves, she guessed.

Trevor also chose more white wine and they began to eat. Once again, Kate was moved to comment.

"This is delicious," she said after a few mouthfuls. "Where did you get the recipe?"

"I didn't. Made it up." Trevor couldn't help a small smile.

They continued to eat in silence, but after a while Kate began to find it uncomfortable, so attempted conversation. She wanted to say something about Ann having invited the boys round, wondering if she had let anything slip, but settled for a safer subject. "Charlie and Paul told me you went to your parents yesterday. How were they?"

"Fine, in good form. The garden was looking lovely and Dad was great at entertaining the boys. I think they enjoyed the beach too, and they swam."

More silence, broken by Trevor. "Like a bit more? There's plenty."

"Honestly, although it's very good, I confess I'm really…" She took a deep breath, not sure how to put it, then decided to be honest. "I'm too on edge, still too angry with you, too nervous about our future, too confused by your email. I can't face any more food right now. Let's get your explanation over with."

Trevor nodded. "OK. I'm pretty nervous too, to tell the truth. I had to concentrate to stop my hand shaking when I poured the wine." He glanced at Kate, but she didn't react. "I made a chocolate mousse for dessert, but it'll keep till tomorrow. I'll just clear the food away and load the dishwasher, if you'll take the wine and glasses through to the sitting room. I won't be long." He stood. "Would you rather have coffee?"

"Not tonight. Let's just finish the wine." Kate picked up the two glasses and the half-empty bottle and left the room. She pushed the sitting room door open with her shoulder and stood for a moment, admiring the way the low evening sun enriched the green of the grass beyond the windows and gently warmed the room. She saw that Trevor had put the vase of roses on the hearth in front of the fireplace. No avoiding them, she thought, as she set the glasses on a side table then sat down in the same armchair as on that fateful afternoon a year ago. She couldn't relax, however, but perched nervously on the edge of the seat as she waited for Trevor.

Chapter 27

Impatience got the better of Kate and after a minute, she stood and went to the French windows. As she admired the garden, her first thought was that unless it rained soon, they would need to start watering. But then, once again, the realisation of the likely outcome of this horrible situation hit hard: this house would no longer be home, there would be no big garden to admire or water. She was a mixture of anger and tears as she heard Trevor enter the room. She turned to face him.

"How could you! How could you risk losing the wife who loved you, three – yes, three – children who adore you, and all this." Her gesture encompassed the garden and their big comfortable home. She was almost shouting. "And not once but twice. It beggars belief."

Sobbing, she moved towards the door as if to leave, but Trevor caught her wrist before she reached it.

"Stop, Kate. Stop. You have to hear my explanation."

Kate tried to pull away, but he held her firmly until she relaxed and, still sobbing, collapsed onto the sofa. Trevor sat down beside her, putting his arm round her shoulder. Kate made the effort not to pull away. He handed her a clean handkerchief which she accepted, wiping her eyes.

Trevor let his arm drop and moved away a little so that he was facing her. "Listen. Look at those roses and remember what I wrote: I love you, I am not having an affair, and I'm going to tell you everything."

Moved by the urgent appeal in his voice, Kate nodded but didn't look at him.

"Do you remember, last week in the hospital, you demanded an explanation for why I lied to you and the office? I said it was partly your fault, and you hit me." Trevor touched his cheek as if remembering the shock and the sting of the slap.

"How could I forget." Kate still didn't look at him.

"Well, let me explain now. A year ago, in this room, we had that traumatic afternoon when I vented my fury at your affair with Jonathan Markham and accused you of still seeing him. You turned the tables on me by saying you had known about my affair with Nicola and not said anything. That was sobering, both then and now. I admire you hugely for that, for sticking with me when I'd been so foolish." Trevor paused. "I still hurt inside when I remember how I sprang my knowledge of the James and Jonathan thing in front of the counsellor and said I wanted a divorce. I can hardly believe I was so cruel. But – and here I'm getting to the point – then you told me that Nicola had a child the same age as James. I was stunned."

"I remember your face, it was a picture," said Kate, sitting up straighter. "It was obvious you knew nothing about it."

"I certainly didn't, but even as I drove to pick up the boys from Ann's, I began to wonder, was it a boy or was it a girl? Had you said *he* was the same age as James, or *she* was the same age as James? I put it out of my mind, telling myself it really didn't matter, but it kept sneaking back. I didn't dare ask you as I didn't want you to think it was important to me – I knew it shouldn't be.

"I was managing pretty well, but the question still popped up uncomfortably often. Then I had to go to the London office for a few days and, telling myself it wasn't really important, I rang Capital from my hotel and asked for Nicola, saying I was an old friend. I even gave a false name. I honestly don't know what I was thinking of, what I would have done had she answered the phone." Trevor shook his head in disbelief. "But fortunately for me, a man answered. He told me she had married to a colleague called Michael Bryant and left the company. He also said he thought they lived in Wimbledon."

Kate was listening attentively by now, her eyes fixed on Trevor who, by contrast, kept his eyes down, palpably embarrassed.

"I remember my first thought was, I wonder what it's like bringing a child up in London? On my way back home to you that night, on impulse I looked up Wimbledon, SW19 on Google. It was clear that some of it was a wealthy area with wide streets near the common and the All England Tennis Club.

"Don't for a minute think that I was comfortable with this obsession. But it just wouldn't go away, however hard I tried. Next time I had to spend a couple of days in London – a month or two ago – in a quiet moment in the office, I searched for SW19 addresses for 'M. Bryant' in the online telephone directory and on the electoral register. I found three, and one evening, rather than a long solitary dinner in the hotel, I took the tube to Wimbledon and walked to all three."

"I can hardly believe what I'm hearing. How did you manage to be so normal at home?"

"Several times I nearly confessed to you, but either it seemed the wrong moment or I was too embarrassed. How I regret it!" He again shook his head at his foolishness. "Anyway, one address was a small terraced house, no sign of children's stuff, and I decided that, as lawyers, they could probably afford better. The second one was more plausible, and the third was a seriously expensive detached house in a wide tree-lined street with grass verges, near the tennis club." Trevor smiled ruefully as he confessed his thoughts at the time. "I remember wondering, has she done so well for herself? Is my son at some posh private school which we couldn't afford?"

"So, what did you do, knock on the door?" said Kate, ignoring this last admission. Her tone was sarcastic and her eyebrow raised, but her attention was fully on him now.

"Of course not! But I did stand there for a while thinking that perhaps I might catch a glimpse of my son. But all that happened was that an older woman came out, got into the silver Mercedes parked in the driveway and drove out, giving me an odd look as she passed. I was disappointed, but realised how idiotic I'd been, as any children as young as James would be in bed by then, even though it wasn't quite dark yet."

At this point, Trevor took a deep breath and looked straight at Kate. "Now we're up to last week." He reached out and took her hand. She flinched, but didn't withdraw it, sensing that Trevor had reached something he was going to find hard to relate.

"I had decided, maybe illogically – but I really wasn't being very logical by this stage – that the big house was where Nicola and family were living and the older woman maybe a mother-in-law or a posh nanny. I also realised I needed to be outside the house earlier when children would be coming home from school. Back in London last week, I told myself this was my last chance – I honestly, truly, never thought beyond that, never wondered what I would do if I did see the child. Crazy, I know, but it really had taken me over. I rang to tell you I would be working late and told the office I had to leave early to go to a parents' meeting at the school. No problem.

"I got to the house by three. It was hot, so I installed myself under a tree for shade, put my jacket, overnight bag and briefcase down on the grass verge and started reading the evening paper. I hadn't been there long when the same woman drove out and gave me a long hard stare as she passed. Gone to get my son, I thought hopefully, and relaxed for a bit. I heard a police car siren coming down the road – imagine how surprised I was when it stopped beside me and two policemen got out. But I still wasn't worried until they came right up to me."

Trevor stopped for a moment. Releasing Kate's hand, he turned away from her and looked down at his feet. There was a tremor in his voice when he started to speak again.

"I can't tell you how embarrassing it was, standing there with the two policemen clearly finding me suspicious, demanding to know what I was doing there. I said I was waiting for a friend, but I was totally thrown when they said they knew I had been there before, so that made things worse. They demanded to know what I did and who I worked for, went through my briefcase. Then they picked up my overnight bag and tipped everything out onto the grass.

"That wasn't even the worst of it. They made me stand with my legs apart and frisked me thoroughly, in full view of any passing cars. Christ, the humiliation. It hurts just to remember it, never mind talk about it." Trevor still didn't look up. "But I promised to tell you everything."

Kate moved closer to Trevor. She put a finger under his chin and lifted his face so that he couldn't avoid looking at her.

"Thank you. I can't understand how you got so obsessed, and I'm sad that you didn't feel able to tell me. I believe the incident with the policemen. But there's still a big question. When I asked you last week about the grass in your underpants, you didn't have an explanation. Have you just made up this story about the policemen tipping out your things?"

Trevor looked at her horrified. "How could you think that? No, of course not. But when you confronted me with the underpants, my mind just froze. I was overwhelmed by James's accident and you discovering my lies. I couldn't think straight. It was later after you'd gone that I stopped to think the whole thing through, and then I remembered noticing the smell of newly mown grass when I was standing on the verge and thinking how nice it was. You have to believe me, please, for God's sake. I don't know how else to convince you."

Kate couldn't yet bring herself to say she forgave him, but she took his hands in hers and squeezed them gently in acknowledgement of his plea. "Give me a while to absorb all this," she said. "But you've not explained what they suspected you of – and why? And did they just let you go?"

Trevor swallowed. "They demanded an explanation of why I was hanging around there and I said it was too embarrassing to tell them standing in the street, so they let me sit in the back of their car. One of them got in beside me, as if I was a prisoner. I told them about Nicola and the child, and I confessed what I had not told anyone, even you – that I had become obsessed with it. They said it was such an unlikely story that they believed me – even joked about it, which made me feel even more foolish.

"When I asked how they had known I was there, they pointed out a CCTV camera which had filmed me both times. Apparently, the house wasn't even lived in by its owners, Bryant or otherwise, but was rented to some character who thought I was up to no good.

"And just to tell you how shaken I was – when they offered to drive me to the tube to come home, I refused, even though as a boy I would have leapt at the chance to drive in a police car, sirens blazing." Trevor managed a small smile at this point.

Kate smiled in sympathy. Later, her mind would be circling around his story, checking for the truth. But she knew that, at this moment, she was inclined to believe him – damn it, she wanted desperately to believe him. However naive and underhand he had been, he had clearly suffered for it and wanted to be back in the family he so loved. She stood.

"We forgot all about the wine. Would you like some?" She moved to get the bottle and glasses. "I think it's still cold enough."

"Yes, please." Trevor rose to join her and, glasses filled, they raised them silently in recognition of the trauma they had each endured.

"There's one more thing to tell you, a twist to the sad story," Trevor said hesitantly, "and I'm going to need your help."

Chapter 28

Kate's heart sank. What could Trevor mean? What more was there to come? The revelations so far were quite enough to cope with for one evening. Was the new problem going to affect her current willingness – desire – to believe him and work on getting back to normal? Gathering her mental strength and taking a big sip of wine before responding, she looked at Trevor questioningly.

"Do we have to talk about this now, or will it keep until tomorrow?"

"I know it's tough, and I'm miserably aware how much I've hurt and distressed you. I can only say sorry again." Trevor's contrition was clear, his eyes beseeching. "But if I don't explain now, you'll be wondering all night, so let me just explain and we can talk about it tomorrow. We both need time to think – I confess I've kept it out of my mind as much as possible until now. The problem is..." He paused and started again. "Do you remember Horst, an old colleague at Capital? I think you must have met him at various office dos."

Kate nodded, surprised at this turn.

"He's always been a bit overly friendly and, well, crude – though he means well. He had noticed Nicola making advances to me back then, teased me a bit about her. I never let on I'd had a relationship with her, so I was very surprised when he rang me recently to tell me her husband had left Capital and taken a job with Staffords – in the Bristol office, of all places! I was still obsessed with seeing the child then, so you can imagine what mixed feelings I had. As if that wasn't enough, he'd said before that he'd heard she had marriage problems and seemed to think it was funny to suggest she'd be after me again. Crazy. I've no interest at all in Nicola, even less in the idea she might set out to catch me again…" Trevor held his hand across his forehead, part covering his eyes as if to shut out his unhappiness.

Kate sat down again wearily, annoyed at what she saw as the apparent triviality of his concern and the dragging out of this painful evening. Why would he have to see Nicola at all, except perhaps at occasional office parties? Then she realised that the child, too, would be living in Bristol and Trevor might still try to see it.

"So why do you need my help? What on earth do you think I can do?" She couldn't hide her impatience and she began to think her secret hope of a romantic – sexual – reconciliation, like last year's, was becoming unlikely.

"I need your support, at the very least, to stop me from trying to see the child. Now you know it all, I can talk to you and get the strength to resist." He sat down beside her. "You are my rock, the centre of my life and I love you. Say you'll forgive me for being so weak and stupid. I honestly don't know what I would do without you by my side." His voice was breaking as he finished.

Kate couldn't help but be moved, in spite of the increasing evidence that her husband was not as strong a character as she had once believed. She turned to put her arms round him, and he cradled his head against her shoulder. To her surprise, she could feel him trembling. She lifted one hand to stroke his hair.

"I do believe you, I really do, even if I'm still angry and saddened by your deception and lack of willpower. And I'm glad you've finally told me everything – at least, I hope it's everything," she added, with a wry smile he couldn't see.

"Oh, it is, it really is." Trevor sat up and looked her in the eye. "I think – I know – I've learnt my lesson. And with you believing me, life seems possible again. When you went to your parents without a word and wouldn't take my calls, the bottom fell out of my world. If I hadn't been looking after the boys, I don't know what I might have done."

That hit Kate hard. She couldn't really believe what he was hinting but she could imagine him drinking too much and crashing the car. She shuddered at the idea. Taking both his hands in hers, she sat up straight and kissed him lightly on the mouth.

"I do love you, Trevor, in spite of all this. Thank heavens we can put it behind us now – well, except for Nicola being in Bristol – and only move forward. I was heartbroken when I thought we really had come to the end. Now I can expect fifteen roses next June!"

Trevor moved as if to kiss her more deeply, but she pushed him away gently.

"I'm really too wrung through to feel sexy, and I suspect you are too, so let's draw a line there for now. Do you have to go to work tomorrow?"

"I guess I should. But I could text Virginia to say I won't be in until late morning, and we can talk more once the boys are at school – and maybe not just talk!" His eyes twinkled, and he sounded more like his usual self.

Although the reconciliation was not as romantic or sexy as she had perhaps initially hoped, Kate was happy to leave it at that. Standing up, she gathered the glasses and the now-empty wine bottle. "I'm going up to have a bath to relax," she said, heading towards the kitchen. "Do you want one?"

"No, I'll just text Virginia about tomorrow then have a shower. See you in bed."

"I may be asleep by then. Don't wake me."

In fact, Kate was still wide awake when Trevor joined her in bed. She snuggled up to him. "Don't you ever, ever put me through this again." She slapped him playfully then gave him a quick kiss. "I didn't tell you, when I was saying good night to Charlie, he looked worried. I asked him why, and he said, 'Please, be nice to Daddy.' I promised I would." She kissed Trevor quickly again, adding, "I may be even nicer tomorrow," before turning away to sleep.

Chapter 29

It took Kate quite a while to get to sleep – not surprising, she thought, given the intense emotions of the past few days. Was it really only four days since James's accident? It seemed like forever. She tried to lie still so as not to disturb Trevor, although she had a sneaking suspicion he might also be awake. She couldn't face another conversation about helping him overcome his obsession, nor was she ready to initiate sex. She made a conscious effort to relax and was surprised to wake refreshed and see early morning sunshine filtering through the curtains.

Seeing that Trevor was still asleep, she slipped quietly out of bed. After checking that all three boys were still sleeping, she went down to make a cup of tea, listening to Radio 4 as she drank it. After the 7am news headlines, she went up to shower and prepare for the day.

Trevor was already out of bed and showered, his towel tied round his waist. Kate took a second to admire his trim figure. He noticed, grinning his acknowledgement.

"Good morning, darling." Trevor greeted her with a kiss. "I had a moment's panic when I woke and you weren't there, but then I heard the radio – what a relief! I didn't really think you'd left again, but..." He didn't need to say more.

Kate smiled in recognition of his momentary concern. "Can you get breakfast ready while I rouse the boys and make sure they've got everything they need. Are their school things clean?"

"Clean enough. Their shorts were OK on Friday, they've got clean shirts and underwear. I didn't do any washing so you'll – we'll," he quickly corrected himself, "need to do some soon."

Kate, appreciating the change but letting it pass with just a quick smile, nodded then showered and dressed before going to James.

"Sleep well?" she asked as she kissed him awake. "How's the shoulder?"

"OK," he said, rubbing his eyes.

"Do you think you can go to school today if I ask the teachers to make sure you take it easy and don't get into any fights? I think you might be a bit bored at home as Daddy and I have things to do." This with an inward smile.

"Mmm, I want to go. I can tell everyone about the accident and the hospital and the fair and the piglets and the coconuts."

"Good. Get dressed then – let me know if you need any help. You should take the sling to protect your shoulder. Bring it down and I'll help you put it on."

She went across the landing to Charlie and Paul and found both boys up – Charlie reading and Paul busy with his fort.

"Getting dressed time, sweethearts. Daddy's putting breakfast out, so come down as soon as you're ready. Did you have any homework?"

"No! Daddy asked the same, but we don't have homework at weekends. You ought to know by now," Paul said with a cheeky grin. "Is James coming to school too?"

"Yes, he says he's OK and I'll have a word with the teachers. See you downstairs."

Breakfast seemed incredibly normal after the dramas of the weekend – the usual demands for Frosties, cornflakes, toast, pass the milk, descending into peace as the boys ate ravenously.

"I'll take you to school," said Kate as she tidied away the dirty bowls and plates. "Go and wash your hands and comb your hair." The three disappeared obediently. "And brush your teeth!"

she called after them as she went to fetch her handbag and keys. "See you shortly," she said to Trevor as they went to the car.

It was only a short drive; Kate parked nearby and accompanied the boys into the playground, waving Charlie and Paul off into the crowd. The same teacher was on duty as on the day of the accident.

"Good morning, Mrs Martin. Hello, James, back already? Couldn't stay away, eh?"

Kate answered for him. "He was incredibly lucky. It was just mild concussion, cracked ribs and a bruised shoulder. As long as he's careful and wears his sling, it isn't a big problem. If you and the other staff could keep an eye on him at break times, that will be fine – but do call me at home if you think he's too tired or in pain."

"Of course. Come and find your friends, James. They'll be so pleased to see you."

Kate's farewell wave went unnoticed by all three boys, her feelings a mixture of pique and relief that they were so happy and integrated at this local school. Her instinctive preference for a private prep school and Trevor's insistence on a state school had caused their first real disagreement, but she could now admit that her concerns had proved unfounded.

She returned to the car and set off for home, but turned into a quiet side road where she parked, needing time to consider her next talk with Trevor. She found it hard to think constructively. Was Nicola and the child moving to Bristol really a problem? How do you wean someone off an obsession? Was Trevor so weak that he would succumb whatever Kate said or did? Did she believe that Nicola herself was truly no threat? Trevor had been so good at hiding first the beginning of the affair and then the obsession, but Kate hoped she was more alert now and would pick up any clues.

With a sinking heart and a wry smile, Kate realised that the only suggestion she could make right now was counselling, not something that Trevor would easily accept after their last attempt. She just had to believe Trevor was sincere in his promises to put it all behind him.

Back home, to her surprise she heard Trevor mowing the lawn and went out to him.

Trevor switched the mower off. "I saw it badly needed doing, and I felt the need of some physical activity. You weren't there so I decided to do the grass instead." His eyes conveyed an unmistakable message. He put his arm round Kate's shoulders and drew her to him. "The rest of the lawn can wait. Better go indoors – can't be certain the neighbours aren't watching!"

"Bugger the neighbours! Anyway, I suspect poor Sally Wootton" – Kate pointed to the bedroom window of the next-door house – "would get a kick from it. Her husband's away most of the time so I bet she misses it." She turned to face the window and began ostentatiously to undo her blouse.

"Kate Martin! I had no idea you were an exhibitionist at heart! However, I insist you only exhibit to me." Laughing, Trevor scooped her up and marched back into the sitting room, dropping her onto the sofa. "Phew, not as fit as I was – or else you've got heavier."

"Hmmm, age might have something to do with it too. And you know, I do appreciate a nice big soft bed for sex." She pulled herself up, took Trevor by the hand and led him upstairs.

Their love-making was inventive, alternately assertive and tender, healing. Sated, they lay side by side, hand in hand.

"I've been thinking about the Nicola problem," Kate ventured. "Do you want to talk about it now?"

"Not really." Trevor squeezed her hand. "But I know I've got to get to grips with it. I'm hoping just being able to talk to you will help. Maybe this can be the start."

"Maybe. The only idea I had was counselling, but that brings back such horrible memories. I think we should leave it until we see how you get on." She paused. "I've just thought. Is there any chance Horst could have got it wrong about what's-his-name Bryant coming to the Bristol office?"

"Michael Bryant. I doubt it, but I'll talk to the HR department and find out. I don't know which team he would be joining, certainly not working with me or I would have known." He released Kate's hand and sat up, swinging his legs over the side of the bed. "I told Virginia I'd be in around noon, so I'd better get a move on."

He turned back and bent over to kiss Kate. "I love you very much. I promise, with your help, I'm going to put all this behind me."

Chapter 30

It was nearly two hours later when an invigorated Trevor drove into the car park under his office, thankful that as managing director of Staffords in Bristol he had a designated space and didn't have to drive around in circles hoping to find a free spot. His buoyant mood carried him up the steps into the main atrium two at a time. Nodding at the uniformed receptionist at the desk he went straight to the lift and pressed the button for 5, the lowest of Staffords' three floors.

The lift doors opened directly into reception. He had barely stepped out of the lift when he was greeted by an enthusiastic "Good morning, Mr Martin. Virginia said you would be in late. How's your little boy? We heard about the accident."

"Good morning, Sophie." He smiled at the young woman at the front desk. "He's doing remarkably well, thanks. He even went to school this morning. He was so lucky – it could have been very much worse. We don't like to think about it."

"Phew, so glad to hear that. We were all worried for you."

Trevor smiled again and, eschewing the lift this time, took the stairs to the seventh floor. Emerging from the staircase, he almost bumped into a colleague coming the other way.

"Morning, Trevor. How's your son? We were all so sorry to hear about the accident."

"Morning, John. Thanks. He's doing remarkably well. He even went to school this morning. He was very lucky – we don't like to think how much worse it could have been." Trevor suppressed a chuckle, realising he was going to have to repeat this little speech many times that day.

"So pleased to hear it. Catch up with you later," John called over his shoulder as he disappeared down the stairs.

Trevor was accosted by two more colleagues before he reached his office and dodged a third by diving into Virginia's room. She looked up smiling.

"Good morning, Trevor, good to have you in today – what a relief that James is home. I was very pleased to get your message this morning as things are starting to pile up. I've put a list on your desk of calls you need to make and can mostly fill you in on what they're about. But tell me, how is James this morning?"

"Amazingly, he really wanted to go to school. Kate's at home today, so she can collect him early if it's too much for him. So I should be able to be here all afternoon. I'll get straight down to work." He went into his office, pausing briefly to admire the view over Bristol from his window before sitting down at his desk and running his eye over Virginia's list.

He had left the door open and didn't hear Virginia coming in, the carpet muffling the sound of her footsteps. She placed a cup of coffee on his desk. He looked up and mouthed his thanks.

"I'll be going out soon to get a bite for my lunch, just to the sandwich bar round the corner. Can I get you anything while I'm there?" Virginia raised her finely painted eyebrows in question.

"Thanks, I hadn't thought about lunch. So, yes, a cheese and pickle on brown, please, and some sort of cake or chocolate biscuit. I'm not fussed which." He fished in his pocket for his wallet and handed her a ten pound note. "No hurry, the coffee will keep me happy for now. But while you're here, just run through this list with me, could you."

The briefing didn't take long. Left alone, Trevor proceeded to work his way down the list. After a short while he felt a strong urge to call Kate. He dialled her mobile.

"Hi darling, how's it going?" Kate answered immediately.

"Fine, though I'm beginning to feel like a broken record as everyone keeps asking about James. There's a lot of work piling up, but I'll try to get home in time to read to the boys. Can you manage until then?"

"I think so. The school hasn't rung, so James must be coping OK."

"Well, do call if you need me. You and James come before work. Actually, I didn't ring to talk practicalities – I rang to say I love you." He paused. "More than I can say."

"I love you too." Kate's voice was warm, and she blew a kiss down the line. "See you this evening. I'll have supper ready about eight."

"Perfect. Bye, darling." Trevor hung up, smiling, then turned back to the notes he had made on what actions were needed. Some were trivial, some weightier, but one gave him pause. The big deal he had been working on in London was coming to a pivotal stage and would require his presence later that week. An involuntary shudder ran through him, as he remembered the horror and embarrassment of his recent visit to London and its aftermath. Was it really only last week? It felt like a lifetime.

"Damn," he said aloud. "Damn, damn, damn." London was the last place he wanted to go.

Virginia appeared in the doorway. "What's the matter?"

"That deal I was working on in London is hotting up, and I'll have to go there this week. I really don't like leaving Kate with all three while James is still recovering, but I don't think I've a choice. Still, I'll make a few calls and see if I can get out of it."

Virginia smiled sympathetically. "Good luck, but meanwhile here's your lunch and the change."

"Thanks." Trevor shut his door to discourage visitors and went back to his calls. He identified the easy ones, dealt with them quickly, then turned his mind to London. Picking up the phone yet again, he dialled the head office.

"Trevor Martin. Can you put me through to Peter Owen, please."

"Certainly, Mr Martin. How's your little boy? We heard about the accident from Mr Owen who heard from Virginia."

Rolling his eyes but managing a smile, knowing it would be 'heard', Trevor repeated his little speech.

"So glad to hear that. Putting you through now." A brief pause. "Mr Martin for you, Mr Owen."

"Thanks for calling when you've so much on your mind. How's your son? We were all very anxious for you." Peter Owen's oleaginous tone was as irritating as usual.

Trevor forced another smile and managed to make his tale sound fresh, then got straight down to business. "About the Hoffman deal and the meetings this week. I really don't like to leave Kate to cope with a still slightly fragile James and the boys. Do you really need me to be there?"

"We most certainly do. You've got all the background from previous meetings and the vital legal expertise for these contracts."

"How about if I document all the arguments, send them through beforehand and attend by conference call? With the video set-up it's almost as good, and I've a shed-load of work here that needs attending to." Trevor tried to sound more business-like than hopeful.

"Sorry, Trevor, but there'll be several side meetings too that you should be at. I reckon we'll need at least two days." Peter's voice was firm. "See you Thursday, 9am."

Trevor knew when he was beaten. "OK, Peter. I'll get to work on it right away."

It was head down for the rest of the afternoon, Trevor barely registering the passing of time until Virginia knocked and put her head round the door.

"Bye, Trevor, I've got to go promptly. See you tomorrow."

"OK, Virginia, have a good evening." Glancing at his watch, he added, "I'll be in early as I don't want to stay late tonight. It's already past five, and I want to be home to spend time with the boys before bed. The weekend was a bit fraught." That's an understatement, he thought to himself.

It was only after Virginia had left that he realised he hadn't given a thought to Michael Bryant's apparent appointment to Bristol and therefore Nicola's and the child's likely proximity. Tomorrow will do, he reassured himself.

Chapter 31

It was almost six when Trevor made his way down to the car park. Although his mood was not as buoyant as that morning, he was still cheerful, knowing he had put in a good afternoon's work and was on his way home to his family.

The traffic was flowing well, he saw with relief as he drove out, but he was surprised to find it was raining quite hard; he had been so absorbed in his work that he hadn't even noticed the rain battering the office windows. He switched on the news, commenting out loud sarcastically at some politicians' sayings and doings. He was pleased to hear the Footsie 100 index was up a little, sorry that the English cricket side were not doing better.

By the time he got home, the rain had become torrential and a strong gusty wind was blowing. Even in the short distance to the front door, he got soaked. Opening the door, he called out.

"Kate, I'm here, just going to take my wet jacket off." He hung it in the laundry room, meeting Kate as he emerged. He held his arms wide and she moved close to be enfolded for a deep kiss.

"My, you really did get wet." She put her hand to his wet hair and smoothed it to one side. "The boys are watching TV. They've had supper."

"How's James? Did he cope OK?"

"Amazingly well, it seems, but he's very tired. He needs to get to bed soon."

Trevor found the boys snuggled up together on the sofa.

"Hello, boys. Room for a little one?" He made to sit beside them.

Charlie and Paul looked up and held a finger to their lips, indicating with their eyes that James was asleep between them.

"Is it OK to chat now, or shall I wait until the programme's over?" Trevor whispered, a courtesy he had learnt from his father who hated to be talked to while he was listening to the radio or TV.

"Now's OK, it's a silly programme – for girls," Paul snorted.

"No, it's not," Charlie retorted. "I like it."

"Then you're a girl."

"You're just stupid."

Trevor sighed. As an only child, he had never had to cope with this sibling bickering. However, his desire to remonstrate was thwarted as James was roused by the noise.

"Hello, Daddy. I went to school today. Everyone wanted to know about the accident."

"Did your shoulder hurt much? Could you join in at break times?"

"Only hurt a little bit. And Charlie and Paul looked after me at lunchtime, and the dinner lady gave me an extra helping of custard."

"That was nice of her. Anyway, how about you and I go upstairs now for a bath and story. I'll read to you two later." He planted kisses on their heads.

All three boys asleep or reading in bed, Trevor came downstairs and joined Kate in the kitchen.

"What lovely roses!" Trevor bent to smell the colourful bunch in a bowl on the table.

"So they should be – they're from your rose bed! I heard there was stormy weather coming so I picked some before they spoiled. The ones you sent me are still gorgeous too." Kate walked round the table to kiss him. "Let's eat.

"So, how was your day? Was there a lot of work piled up?"

"Yes, though some of it I could deal with quickly. But," Trevor looked up at Kate. "I'm afraid I've got to go to London for two days at the end of this week. The Hoffman deal has got to a critical stage and they want me there. I called Peter Owen and tried to get out of it, said I'd join by video call, but he was adamant. I'm very sorry."

Kate hid any disappointment. "I'm sure I can cope – after all, it's nothing new."

"But I really don't like leaving you, with James still recovering." He looked down at his plate. "And to be honest, the trauma of last week is so fresh, and the idea of going anywhere near London fills me with horror, even though I know it's irrational." He held out his hand across the table, reaching for Kate, who took it in both of hers.

"It's not that you're going to be stalking women in Wimbledon this time." Kate managed a small smile. "You promised me faithfully that you had put this behind you." She paused. "But you did say you would find out what's happening with this Michael Bryant appointment. Did you learn anything?"

Embarrassed but also relieved that he hadn't thought about it all day, Trevor confessed he had forgotten about it in the pressure of work, and Virginia had gone home by the time he remembered. "I'll ask her tomorrow. Did you have a relaxed day once the boys were at school?"

"Well," Kate looked him directly in the eye and her voice had a hard edge to it. "There was the clothes washing and house tidying from the weekend – Mrs Evans doesn't come until Wednesday – and shopping and cooking..."

"Sorry." Trevor had the grace to look contrite. "Honestly, I do appreciate how you keep the house running so smoothly, really I do."

"Well, don't take it for granted." Kate did not sound entirely mollified. "Actually, I also rang your parents to thank them for looking after you all on Saturday and to tell them how well James is doing. I know I've said it before, but they really are sweeties. We must have them over soon. Then I called my mother. I think she realised there was something wrong at the weekend, but she was immensely tactful, bless her, not always her strong point. I think she's reassured now."

Glad to have diverted the conversation from his London visit and the Bryants, Trevor cleared the dirty plates and served the chocolate mousse they hadn't eaten the night before. He broached a new topic.

"We've not done anything about the summer holidays, though we did vaguely talk about camping in France. What do you think?"

"I like the idea, and I'm sure the boys would too. We've left it rather late to book a hotel or cottage, so let's plan on that," Kate said over her shoulder, as she stood to put the kettle on for coffee. "Why don't you go and relax in the sitting room, and I'll join you in a minute."

When she entered with the coffee, she found Trevor ensconced on the sofa. He patted the cushion beside him, took the mugs from her and put them safely on the side table. Kate sat down and he moved closer, putting his arm around her shoulder.

"Actually, it's you I want right now," he whispered in her ear. One hand slid down to fondle her breast, while the other somehow found its way to her knee and crept higher under her skirt. "The coffee can wait."

Kate offered no resistance as he continued his exploration of her body; he had learnt well over the years of their marriage just what touch she most enjoyed, and she soon became as aroused as he was. Entwined, they tumbled to the floor, shedding clothes as they fell.

"My God, Trevor Martin, you do know how to get a girl excited." Kate gasped, casting a quick glance at the door to make sure there were no boys observing their activity.

"Oh, but it has to be the right girl," Trevor responded as he nibbled her ear, then kissed her all the way from her nose to her

toes, lingering at sensitive points in between. Kate responded in kind and they climaxed satisfyingly and noisily.

"Lucky this is a big solid house," Kate laughed as they calmed down. "I bet in some modern boxes we'd have woken the boys."

Trevor was able to put London out of his mind as they lay there together, relaxed and happy. "I love you. Thank you again for believing me and coming home yesterday. I truly don't know what I would have done if you hadn't."

"But I did. And I love you. And I don't want any coffee. Bedtime!" Kate started to get to her feet then stopped, kneeling, and looked down at Trevor, naked, still prone on the floor. "When did we last make love twice in one day?" She touched his lips with her fingers. "Good to know we're not past it yet!"

Laughing, they took the untouched coffee to the kitchen and went upstairs to bed. Relaxed and ready for a good night's sleep, Trevor found his was delayed by a troubling thought lurking at the back of his mind. He tried to place it. Get a girl excited? He groaned, causing Kate to turn and mutter in her sleep. It was Nicola who had once said that. Unbidden, his mind conjured up the occasion: a steamy summer afternoon, a cheap hotel room in London, rumpled bedclothes. *No, please, no! I don't want to remember.* He forced himself to turn his thoughts to work, to the summer holiday, anything but Nicola naked, spread-eagled on the tangled sheets.

Chapter 32

Trevor made an early start at the office. To his relief, his morning was relatively tranquil. Word had clearly spread that James was in no danger, so Trevor was spared the repetition of his little speech; passing colleagues just waved or smiled to acknowledge his return, and by the time Virginia brought in his mid-morning coffee, he had dealt with the remaining queries from the day before and was ready to start on the Hoffman papers.

The thought of the London visit reminded him all too forcefully of his promise to Kate. He smiled at Virginia as she placed the mug on his desk.

"Thanks, I'm ready for that. By the way, I meant to mention yesterday that I've heard a rumour on the grapevine that Michael Bryant from Capital, my previous company, has taken a job with us here. Could you possibly check it out for me? HR will know – don't know why I wasn't informed before. I expect to be told about all new professional recruits, however junior."

"Certainly, Trevor, no problem." Virginia was her usual competent self, punctilious in the performance of her duties. Her below the knee skirts and modest blouses set her somewhat apart from the younger secretaries and from the junior women lawyers, who mostly wore trousers and more fashionable tops. He would have laughed if he had known that Kate had once wondered if there was a relationship between them.

Trevor watched her leave, suppressing a frisson of prurient interest in the outcome of his enquiry, sparked by last night's brief memory of Nicola, then turned to his papers, breaking only to get a breath of fresh air and stretch his legs fetching a sandwich from the nearby deli.

"I've got the information you requested." Virginia was standing in the doorway.

He had been so absorbed in the challenging niceties of the deal, he had forgotten the question and looked up surprised.

"Michael Bryant."

"Oh, yes. What did you find out?"

"He is joining us, in the Litigation department under Mr Evinson. Starts quite soon, first of July."

"Thanks, Virginia. Nothing else for the moment – unless you've something for me?"

"No, all quiet. Let me know if you need me. Meanwhile, I'll get your rail tickets on your phone and book the usual hotel. What time do you need to be in the office?"

"Early, unfortunately. By 9am latest. I hope to get away on time Friday evening. But get the flexible tickets as usual, just in case. Thanks."

Virginia nodded and turned to leave, but Trevor called her back.

"One thing: Kate and I are planning our summer holiday with the boys. Could you please confirm the dates I logged, so I can check I put them in my diary correctly."

"I happened to see the schedule yesterday. You booked the second two weeks of August." Virginia smiled and left.

Trevor returned to his papers, refusing to think about any M. Bryants.

Home in good time, he was met by an excited Kate.

"Guess what! My sister has just emailed to invite us to stay with them in Cape Cod this summer holiday! They've taken a big cottage in a resort for the whole of August. What do you think? Can we afford it?"

“I thought we were going camping in France? We agreed the boys would love it.” Trevor sounded petulant. He found he was surprisingly disappointed, realising how much he had been looking forward to it. The physicality and simplicity made such a change from his office life.

Kate’s face fell, but then she rallied. “Surely the boys would be really excited by going to America and seeing their cousins?”

“I’m not sure,” Trevor prevaricated. “It would be expensive and I’ve only booked two weeks off; it’s a long way to go for two weeks.”

“Oh, come on, you’ve done lots of long-distance business travel for shorter stays.”

“Yes, but it’s no fun,” Trevor responded grumpily.

“That’s not the same. Please, think about it. It’s such an opportunity, and we don’t see Fiona and Todd very often. The resort sounds terrific – lots of things for the kids to do together. I’ve forwarded her email to you. Have a look and let’s talk about it over supper.”

“OK, but don’t mention it to the boys. I’m not promising anything,” Trevor said firmly before going to say hello to his sons.

“Got any homework this evening?” he addressed Charlie and Paul. “Anything you need help with?”

“I’ve done mine,” said Charlie smugly before disappearing into his room. Paul admitted he was finding his maths tricky, so the two sat down in Trevor’s study to puzzle through it together. James looked over their shoulders for a while but soon gave up and went off to play.

Trevor had time to look at Fiona’s email before joining Kate in the kitchen. He had to admit the resort looked fun and the cottage very comfortable. He googled Cape Cod: abundance of good beaches, sand dunes and other attractions for the boys. His view mellowed, though the appeal of camping was still strong. The cost of the flights for the five of them was discouraging, but at least they wouldn't be paying for accommodation.

He didn't want to seem to give in too easily so waited for Kate to start the conversation.

"Well, have you had any thoughts?" Kate looked up hopefully from her plate of fish pie. "I do think it would be a shame to pass up such an opportunity."

Trevor finished his mouthful before replying. "Yes, I have – and this is delicious, by the way," indicating the pie. "The resort does look fun. I checked flights – expensive, but not outrageous, and given we don't pay for the cottage, bearable, I think."

Kate looked surprised at his quick capitulation but smiled her gratitude.

"I didn't say yes," Trevor emphasised, teasingly. "I only meant that I'd think about it some more. I still really like the idea of camping with the boys, if not in France, then here, maybe Wales or Cornwall."

"Well," Kate countered. "I've been thinking too. How about this for an idea: why not do both and..."

"But I've only got two weeks scheduled, as I said," Trevor interrupted.

"Wait, you haven't heard my idea – actually two ideas. You – we – could camp for maybe four or five days, come home, then fly over to spend the rest of your two weeks with Fiona and Todd. I know it's even shorter, but you would get your camping. Second idea, you could come home, and the boys and I could stay another few days, even a week. Really good for the boys to get to know Pearl and Dane."

She saw Trevor roll his eyes and laughed. "I bet there are funnier names in their classes."

"Let me think about it and look into the actual cost. I promise I'll take your ideas seriously."

"Thank you, darling." Kate went round the table to give Trevor a hug.

Trevor seized the moment to give his news. “I got Virginia to check the Michael Bryant situation. He is coming to Staffords, starting first of July. He’ll be working for the Litigation department, so there’ll be no need for our paths to cross.”

Kate gave him a kiss. “Be strong,” she whispered in his ear. “You promised.”

Reflecting on their conversation as she settled down to sleep that night, Kate had a sudden doubt about leaving Trevor on his own in Bristol as she had suggested. Could she be sure he would keep his promise to stop trying to see his child or, even worse, that he wouldn’t seek out Nicola and try to resume their relationship? Had she inadvertently laid temptation in his way? He had been adamant that he had put his obsession behind him, but he had deceived her before.

She sighed and turned over grumpily, cross with herself for introducing her doubts but aware she would inevitably be horribly vigilant, watching and listening for every unusual excuse, every nuance in his speech.

Her sudden movement and sigh roused Trevor. “You OK?” he murmured sleepily, reaching out to touch her shoulder.

“Mmmm, of course. Sorry I disturbed you.” She stroked his hand lightly and curled up away from him. “Sleep well.” But she didn’t go straight to sleep herself, as a thought passed through her mind about how she might help ease Trevor’s obsession with his child.

Chapter 33

Home in good time from the office next day, Trevor dropped his briefcase on the floor outside his study. It landed with such a thud that Paul, who had heard the car pull up and rushed down to greet his father, tried to lift it.

"Golly, that's heavy. What's in it?"

"Only my laptop and a big pile of papers for some meetings in London. Paper is very heavy and dense. Architects designing libraries have to include specially reinforced floors." An opportunity for a little learning.

Keen to show off his new knowledge, Paul followed Trevor to the kitchen where Kate was preparing supper. "Mum, did you know that paper is so heavy, libraries have to have special floors? You should feel Dad's briefcase."

"No, darling, I didn't, that's really interesting." Kate smiled as she turned to give Trevor a welcoming kiss. "I'm afraid I've done nothing about packing your overnight bag yet but there'll be time later – or I could do it now if you take over preparing the vegetables."

"Not to worry. I really ought to pack it myself, but you're so much better than me at folding shirts – maybe you could give me a shirt-folding lesson after supper." This was said with an unmistakable twinkle. "But now, if you don't mind, I'll go and spend some time with the boys before supper. Come on, Paul, let's join the others. I can hear them upstairs."

Kate turned back to the supper preparations with just a wry smile.

Later, over supper, Trevor apologised to the boys that he wouldn't see them in the morning and would be in London for a couple of days – maybe Friday evening as well. "But I'll be home all weekend, so there's time to think about what we might do."

All three boys fed and in bed, Trevor and Kate lingered companionably over coffee. As they finished, Trevor stood and held out a hand to Kate. "Why don't you give me that shirt-folding lesson now?" He led the way up to their room.

Rather than getting a shirt out, Trevor playfully draped his big jacket over Kate's slim frame and insisted she tried walking in his office shoes, whereupon she fell over her own feet. Laughing, Trevor put out a hand to save her, and they tumbled together onto the floor in a jumble of that day's clothes, the shirt to be folded still hanging reproachfully in the open wardrobe.

"I'll do it this time," Kate grinned as, recovered from the energetic sex, they picked themselves up and began to get ready for bed. "But don't count on me in future! What time's your train?"

"Some ungodly hour, the 6.33 from Temple Meads I think." He fished out his phone and checked the ticket. "Yes, and Virginia's ordered a taxi for 5.45. I'll put my stuff in the spare bedroom and try not to disturb you. I'll have breakfast on the train."

"Thanks, that's thoughtful. You have first turn in the bathroom, I'm in no hurry."

In bed, they contented themselves with a kiss and a cuddle.

"See you Friday evening, probably after nine but I'll call if I'm going to be earlier. We'll talk about the holiday over the weekend." Trevor turned his light out while Kate, not feeling ready for sleep, settled with her Kindle.

Kate slept through Trevor's careful departure and woke to the normal morning routine. The boys safely delivered to school, she sat down at the kitchen table for a leisurely coffee. Gazing out of the window, she admired the light on the trees, the leaves not yet tired from the summer sun. On impulse, she took her coffee into the garden and stood in the sunshine. It must have rained in the night, she thought, as the air smelled sweetly of grass and roses.

Kate realised how the stress of the past week had taken its toll and how tired she was. She resolved to relax but decided to start with a gentle run on the Downs while the day was still young.

There were few people about, and Kate revelled in the peace, allowing her mind to go where it would as she ran. Inevitably, however, it soon returned to the Nicola/child/Michael Bryant problem. Her embryonic plan seemed plausible, but there was nothing she could do until Michael Bryant started work – there was no other way she could track him down. Forcing her mind off this, she reflected that she had done nothing about a possible Open University course. One thought had been science, but as she rounded the last corner and set off for home, she realised she had lost all enthusiasm for it.

"I must do something," she told herself out loud. "I don't want to sit at home letting my perfectly good brain get lazy." Kate stopped short, suddenly realising that in the drama of James's accident, she had forgotten all about her shift at the Millcrest charity shop. Embarrassed, she made a mental note to ring to apologise.

Kate was always surprised by how easy it was to let time slip by when there were no specific tasks to be done. It was almost noon before she got round to putting some effort into the day. She decided to invite Trevor's parents for Sunday lunch; they would certainly want to see James, having heard about the accident and been so good with Charlie and Paul while she was at her parents. She rang them and they were predictably delighted to come. She was relieved there was no hint of their having felt neglected. Ten minutes on the phone to her own parents brought them up to date and further reassured her mother that all was well.

"Fiona has invited us to stay with them in Cape Cod in August. They've rented a place for a month in a big resort with all sorts of facilities – sounds terrific. Trevor had wanted to go camping, but I think he'll come round, as it's such a special opportunity."

"Sounds exciting – and very generous. I hope Trevor does agree – he certainly should!" Her mother's tacit allusion to the recent marital rift.

After lunch, Kate decided to check out the OU courses before going to fetch the boys. She was just setting up her laptop when the phone rang.

"Hello, Kate Martin."

"Hello, Kate. It's Marjorie from the Millcrest charity shop. I was just wondering if you were coming in this week, as…"

"Oh, God! Oh, I'm so sorry, Marjorie. I was going to ring you to apologise – I only remembered this morning that I'd let you down. I completely forgot last week, as James…"

Marjorie interrupted her. "It's OK, Kate. We understand and honestly would have been surprised if you had come in, as we knew about the accident. One of your neighbours who's a regular customer came in. She told us what had happened."

"Still, I feel very bad about not letting you know, but it completely slipped my mind in all the drama."

"Don't worry about it, but do tell me, how is your son? I hope it wasn't too serious."

Kate told the story and apologised again. "I will be in as usual tomorrow, don't worry. Thank you for being so understanding."

"No problem. I look forward to seeing you tomorrow. Oh, by the way, there's something I want to talk to you about. Have you got two minutes?"

"Yes, I don't have to collect the kids for a while yet."

"I've been asked by one of the Millcrest trustees if I know of anyone in Bristol who might consider joining our board. I thought of you, knowing how much you've helped us, in the shop and editing our newsletter. And as you have three sons, I imagine you can identify with our focus on making sure all young people develop their potential. What do you think?"

"Gosh, that's out of the blue." Kate paused. "I certainly believe strongly in what Millcrest does, but I don't know anything about being a trustee, what it entails. I can't believe I'd be of any use. And anyway, wouldn't meetings be in London?"

"No, the head office is in Bristol. And the reason for thinking of you is that we've all admired your editing of the newsletter. You write very well and could be very helpful in our communications strategy. But you don't have to decide right now. Have a think about it and maybe google the Charity Commission website for guidance on trusteeship. We'll talk more tomorrow in the shop. The trustee who approached me says she could come in to meet you. Then, if you're interested in taking it forward, you could attend a board meeting to see how we work."

"I'm flattered, but... well, I'll do a bit of research and see you tomorrow. Thank you anyway."

"OK, bye for now." Marjorie hung up.

Returning to her laptop, Kate dithered between looking up charity trustee responsibilities or OU courses. Deciding on the former, she found plenty of information, none of it too off-putting. Hmm, she thought to herself, it's certainly worth talking to them. It's gratifying they're interested in me.

Turning to the OU website, she scrolled through the list of courses. Art History? No. Business and Management? No. Computing and IT? No. Childhood and Youth Studies? Ah, that might be worth investigating. She continued down the list, skipping quickly past Engineering, Law, Philosophy but stopping at Psychology and Counselling. Reading a little more, she began to wonder whether this might be both interesting and a possible route into work other than teaching. Plus, she thought with a wry smile, she had a little experience on the receiving end and, if things had taken a different course in their marriage, it might have become a bigger part of her life. Maybe the past year would help her with insights for other couples. However, she was disconcerted to see that, studying part time, it would take several years. That gave her pause.

Glancing at her watch, she saw it was nearly time for the boys and left more research for later.

Trevor called in the evening and again the next afternoon. "Sorry, I shan't be home before at least nine," he apologised. "Don't bother about supper. Virginia got first-class tickets as usual, so there'll be dinner on the train – not up to your standard, but I'll live." Kate could hear his smile.

"I've had a surprise offer." Kate wanted to share her news. "Millcrest are interested in having me as a trustee!"

"That sounds worth following up. Well done, but tell me about it tonight. Must go. Apologise to the boys for me. Love you."

"Love you."

Over supper, she and the boys planned Saturday's activities: a visit to the zoo and maybe a swim too. "But we must let Daddy have a bit of a lie-in, as he'll be tired. There'll still be time for everything. And on Sunday Nana and Pops are coming to lunch. Let's hope the weather's nice so we can have a barbecue – and you can help."

It was well past nine when Kate heard Trevor's key in the lock and the familiar thud as his briefcase hit the floor. She went to the hall to meet him, exchange kisses and a hug.

"All well?" Kate asked as they went to the kitchen. "Coffee?"

"Yes, please. But I confess I'm pretty tired. The meetings were good, very constructive but demanding. It's all quite exciting." He paused. "I'm afraid I'm going to have to go to Germany, maybe for a couple of weeks, probably very soon. I'm really, really sorry to leave you for so long, but I don't think there's any way round it. The deal is getting to the final stages, and the legal niceties will be quite tricky. Face to face at this stage is important."

Kate tried to hide her disappointment but was only partially successful. Trevor apologised again and cheered her up with his decision: "I promise this won't spoil our holiday plans. In fact, I've decided I think you're right that we should go to Fiona and Todd. It's a fantastic offer and will be a real change. Camping can wait for another time."

"OK, I know you have no choice about Germany, but I'm delighted you agree to Cape Cod. Thank you, darling." Kate smiled at the prospect.

Trevor yawned. "I'll skip coffee after all and have a quick bath and go to bed, if you don't mind. See you upstairs later – if I'm still awake. I can hardly keep my eyes open! And tell me all about Millcrest tomorrow." Trevor blew her a kiss and left the room.

Kate's disappointment was soon lessened by the realisation that not having Trevor around when Michael Bryant started work at Staffords might actually help her plans along.

Chapter 34

Saturday was busy with excursions to the Downs, with Ann and family, and to a local swimming pool. Trevor's parents came to a barbeque lunch on Sunday, his father presiding over the chicken and sausages with his usual competence, and the boys kept busy fetching and carrying from the kitchen to the garden. It was quite late in the afternoon before Kate and Trevor were able to sit down in the sitting room and catch up with their respective weeks and concerns; Trevor's parents had left, the boys were playing in the garden.

"Tell me about the Millcrest trustee invitation." Trevor opened the conversation.

"I had a long talk with one of the existing trustees, Christine Peverell…"

"I know her husband," Trevor broke in. "He's a partner in one of the big accountancy firms here. Nice man – lives in Redland, I think."

"Well, she's nice too, and she made the idea of being a trustee sound quite attractive and not too scary. She explained about trustee official responsibilities and talked about what trustees do and how they can contribute to the charity."

"So, do you think it's something you'd like to take on? I think it's a great charity, and you'd be good at it. You've supported and helped them for several years, with the newsletter, not just in the shop."

"Yes, I'm quite excited by the idea, actually. It seems they think I would be useful with their communications strategy – said they like my writing. I've agreed to meet another trustee or two, and then perhaps attend a board meeting before I have to decide." Kate smiled happily. "But tell me more about this German trip. When does it start and where will it be? Berlin?"

"No, the company's in Dusseldorf and it'll probably be the last week of June or possibly the first week of July. It's about a two-week job as I said, but I can come home for the weekend in the middle."

"That's good. And you won't miss any of the school holidays, as I double-checked and they don't break up until the 24th of July." Kate didn't mention that she had looked particularly to see how much time she had before Trevor's return in which to pursue her Michael Bryant plan.

******

The Dusseldorf visit indeed began at the end of June. As July 1st, the date Michael Bryant was due to start at Staffords, drew close, Kate thought more deeply about her plan. Once Trevor had left for Dusseldorf, she rang Virginia to enlist her help.

"Good morning, Virginia. Kate Martin."

"Oh, hello, Kate. Good to hear from you. What can I do for you?"

"Well, you may know Michael Bryant has come to work for Staffords. His wife used to be a colleague of Trevor's in his previous company, and I thought it might be a nice surprise for Trevor to arrange for us all to meet up as a sort of welcome to Bristol." Kate was glad she wasn't having this conversation face to face, as she feared her guilt at the deception would be visible.

"That's a kind thought. I'm sure it would be much appreciated." Virginia's response was warm. "But how can I help?"

"I thought you might ask HR how to contact him for me. He'll have moved to Bristol already, I think. Ideally, I'd like his address as well as a phone number, as I'll put the invitation in writing as a first step."

"I'll see what I can do. I'll call you when I've got anything to report."

"Thanks, Virginia, that's great. Oh – you won't mention it to Trevor, will you. I would like to surprise him, as I said."

"No problem. I'll get on to HR now – I'm not quite so busy with himself away!"

"Thanks, a million. I'll wait to hear. Bye." Kate hung up, not surprised to find she was trembling. This was a big step she was taking, and quite a risk.

Virginia called back that same afternoon.

"Hello, Kate. I've got the information you wanted. Got something to write on to hand?"

"Just a second." Kate reached across the table for her shopping list pad and pen. "OK, fire away."

"I only have a mobile number for him." Virginia read it out. "He's living in 4 Castleton House, 24 Castleton Road. It's in St Andrews – not as nice as Clifton or Redland perhaps, but handy for Gloucester Road, and there's a big park too."

"Any mention of the family at all?"

"No, just the details I've given you and his CV."

"Thanks, Virginia, you're a star. No wonder Trevor talks so highly of you." Kate thought a little flattery wouldn't go amiss and, anyway, it was true. "Bye, enjoy the peace and quiet while you can!"

"Will do. Bye."

As she hung up, Kate was suddenly struck by the address. 4 Castleton House sounded like a flat. Unless it was a big flat with a garden, it seemed improbable as a family home. Intrigued, she decided to investigate before taking her plan any further. She glanced at her watch – just time to go and have a look before picking up the boys.

It was only a ten-minute drive until she turned into Castleton Road, her eyes scanning the numbers as she drove slowly along the pleasant street of mostly semi-detached, grey stone, turn-of-the-century houses like so much of that part of Bristol. 18, 20, 22 – yes, the neat houses were interrupted by a modern block of flats, low-rise, quite pleasant and well maintained but not at all special. Castleton House was painted over the lintel of the archway leading through to a car park behind. Kate parked a little further up the street and walked back. Feeling rather self-conscious, she approached the block and found the entry bells under the arch. Running her eye down them she saw that, although most of the bells had names beside them as well as numbers, number four was blank.

Maybe he hasn't got round to putting his name in, she thought, since he's only just moved here. But number four can't be ground floor – that would be one and two. So, no garden. She glanced around to make sure there was no-one about and continued through the arch to the car park from where she could see the ground floor flats had small patio gardens, the upper ones modest balconies. She turned and walked back to the car, pondering why a lawyer, presumably reasonably well paid and with a family, wasn't living in a house.

Ah, of course! Probably he's just renting until he can move the family here. Damn, that might mean a slight change of plan. No, the original idea still works.

Kate got back into the car and drove to pick up the boys.

Chapter 35

Trevor rang from Dusseldorf early enough to talk to the boys before bedtime. Kate put the phone on loudspeaker and as they gathered around, he told them that Germany, like the rest of Europe, was an hour ahead of the UK and so he would be in bed not long after them. They found this very amusing.

"Why isn't Britain the same?" asked Charlie.

Trevor started to explain about European time being an hour different from ours, and the sun setting earlier nearer the equator in summer, but he could sense their lack of understanding. "I'll explain when I'm home at the weekend, but I'll tell you one thing about it. The UK did discuss moving to the same time as Europe, but the farmers in Scotland refused as they said the cows wouldn't like being milked in the dark!"

"Aren't they milked in the dark in the winter anyway?" Charlie was on the ball.

Trevor, impressed, was momentarily silenced, then continued. "Well said, m'lad! People aren't always logical – I expect you'll learn that in time."

"What, even you?" This was Paul the irrepressible.

Trevor laughed and turned to easier topics.

Kate was happy to let them chat and stuck to banalities when it was her turn. "Was the flight OK? Have they put you in a decent hotel?"

"Yes and yes. The hotel's very comfortable and it's even got a hot tub on the roof. As I'll be here a while, I think I'll go and buy swimming trunks – I know the Germans are pretty hot on nudity but somehow I doubt it's appropriate here. Must go, sorry, I'm meeting a couple of the home team for dinner. Love you."

"I love you too," said Kate, meaning it wholeheartedly but aware that she was acting behind his back on the Nicola/Michael Bryant saga. "Talk tomorrow?"

"Of course. Same time. Bye for now."

******

Kate was on duty at the Millcrest charity shop next morning, glad of something to stop her dwelling on the phone call she planned to make that afternoon. There were quite a few customers, some of whom she knew who wanted to hear about the accident and be reassured that all was now well, so the time passed quickly.

Sitting down with a coffee after lunch, she opened her laptop to read the news but realised she was subconsciously procrastinating. Come on, she said to herself, don't put it off, it won't get any easier.

She reached for the phone and retrieved the paper with Michael Bryant's number. Even as she began to dial, she castigated herself for not thinking straight. He would surely think it odd that she had his private number. She put the phone down and sat thinking for a minute, before deciding that phoning the office would anyway be better – more business-like.

The butterflies with which she was becoming uncomfortably familiar were fluttering wildly in her stomach as she dialled Staffords' number and asked to speak to Michael Bryant.

"Which department would that be?" the female voice asked politely.

Kate had to think rapidly. "Er, legal." Then racking her brains to remember what Trevor had told her, "Litigation, I think. He's quite new," she added as if that would help. Her nervousness must surely be audible, she felt.

"Oh, yes, putting you through."

"Thank you." God, these butterflies must be monarchs at least, she thought.

"Michael Bryant."

The voice was neutral, pleasant, quite deep. Kate swallowed and forced herself to smile.

"Hello, I'm Kate Martin, Trevor Martin's wife. Trevor used to work at Capital, I don't know if you knew him then?"

"No, the name doesn't ring a bell – oh, wait. Not Trevor Martin, the managing director here?"

"Yes, that's my husband. He heard from a friend that you were joining Staffords and that you had married Nicola who used to be his assistant." So far, so outwardly calm.

There was silence for a moment. Kate rushed to fill it, her nervousness making her talk faster than usual.

"Well, I thought it would be nice to welcome you both to Bristol. Trevor's away at the moment – he's in Germany on some big deal – Dusseldorf – he's away for a couple of weeks – I'm sure he would – so would you like to – I think – I thought I could arrange it for when…" Kate realised she was barely making sense and stopped mid-sentence, embarrassed.

"Sorry, I'm not sure I got that." His reply was very diplomatic.

Kate almost literally pulled herself together, sitting up straighter and forcing herself to calm down. She thought briefly of making an excuse for herself – sorry, I was distracted by a wasp circling round me – but decided it would sound unlikely and just make things worse.

"Sorry, let me start again. I – we – would like to invite you and Nicola round for a drink, to welcome you to Bristol and to Staffords, and to renew acquaintance with Nicola. I knew her slightly too." There, it was done.

Another silence before he replied. His voice took on a harder tone, not exactly angry, but definitely sharper.

"No, thank you all the same."

Kate was disconcerted. He really didn't sound friendly, but he had been so abrupt, the change of tone made her curious. She decided to persevere.

"Oh, are you sure? Really? Trevor will be so disappointed." Lying through her teeth.

"No, thank you."

Without thinking, nerves forgotten, Kate continued to press him. "That's a pity. But why won't you come? It would be very informal – just the two of you, not a party."

"If you really want to know, Mrs Martin, Nicola has left me. I'm here on my own."

Kate, suddenly relieved at the apparent removal of Nicola from the picture, was about to offer some words of sympathy when Michael began to speak again, this time his voice almost cracking with emotion.

"She's taken our son to join his father."

Kate froze. Please God this can't be Trevor's worst deception ever. Surely Nicola hasn't left her husband to join Trevor in Dusseldorf! She remembered that it was in Germany that the affair had started. Completely overcome, she started to cry, forgetting that Michael Bryant was still on the line.

"Sorry, I didn't need to tell you that, very unprofessional. It just slipped out – I've not told anyone before, but your invitation threw me."

Kate didn't hear his apology. As her sobs grew quieter, Michael spoke again.

"Are you all right?" His voice had reverted to its kinder tone. "What have I said to upset you?"

"It's complicated." Kate managed to speak fairly coherently. "Look, please can we talk away from the office. I think I need to explain but it's very painful for me and, from your reaction, I fear it will be for you too."

"I'm not sure I want to talk about Nicola, especially to her ex-boss's wife and when there's clearly some history to this."

"Please." Her voice was strong and pleading.

"Well…"

"You can come to my house after work, or I can get a childminder and come to your place. Please." Kate was insistent.

"OK." With a sigh, he agreed. "I'm really not happy about it, but it sounds as though it's very important to you. I'm not busy yet as I've only just joined the team, so I don't have to work late. I would prefer you came to my flat unless we could meet in a café somewhere."

"I'd much rather not meet in a public place. I'll come to your flat in…" Kate stopped herself just in time, remembering that he wouldn't like the thought that she had been snooping. "Where do you live?"

Michael gave his address. "Can you get away tomorrow evening?"

Kate thought quickly. She wanted to get this conversation over before seeing Trevor.

Could she get a sitter? Or maybe Ann would have the boys for a sleepover. She could explain the reason, and she knew Ann would do her best to help.

"I think so. Give me your phone number and I'll call this evening or at the office tomorrow morning to confirm."

"Here it is." He gave the mobile number. "But I must say again, I'm not happy about this."

"I realise and I'm very grateful. Thank you. Hopefully we'll talk tomorrow. Bye."

"Goodbye."

Kate sat back, now dry-eyed and angry, though she did realise that perhaps – once again – there was an innocent explanation. She decided to call Ann before trying to engage a babysitter.

Chapter 36

The phone rang several times before Ann answered.

"Hi, Ann, hope I didn't interrupt anything."

"Hi, Kate, no, sorry, I was just in the garden doing some dead-heading. How are you?"

"Honestly, Ann, I don't know. Don't be surprised if I burst into tears."

"Why? What on earth is up? Is it one of the boys? Are you ill?" Ann's voice was full of concern.

"No, nothing like that. I've just been talking to bloody Nicola's husband..."

"You've been doing WHAT? How in heaven's name did that come about?"

"Well, I wanted to try to meet up with them while Trevor was away. I thought that if I could find a way for Trevor to see this child of his without upsetting everyone, it might lay his wretched obsession to rest, so I called Michael Bryant – that's the husband – at the office. I think I told you he's come to work at Staffords."

"So, what did he say?"

"He was reluctant to talk but finally told me Nicola had left him to join the father of her child..." At this point Kate's self-control almost gave way; the effort it took was evident in the hardness of her voice. "It's possible she's gone to join Trevor in Germany. It's where their affair began."

"Oh, God." There was a momentary silence as Ann took this in. "But don't jump to conclusions, you really will make yourself ill. There may be another explanation. Look, I can't talk much right now – it's time to get the boys. I'll call back."

"OK, but can you babysit for me tomorrow evening? Please?" That pleading tone again.

There was a brief pause before Ann replied. "I think so. I'm pretty sure John'll be at home. But right now, why don't I pick up your three with Mike and Peter – there's plenty of room in the car – and we'll come to your house. The boys can play while we talk."

"You're an angel. I'll call the school right away and let them know. Thanks a million. See you soon – I'll put the kettle on. Bye." Kate sighed as she put the phone down. Although she knew that talking to Ann would calm her down, it wouldn't solve any problems.

About half an hour later the doorbell rang, and Kate opened the door to find five excited boys jostling to get in. "We're here!" Ann stated the obvious with a big smile as she followed them into the hall.

"Lovely to see you, Mike and Peter – it's been a while since you came here after school. How about milk and biscuits in the kitchen before you go to play?"

There was no need to ask twice. Refreshed, the boys chased each other upstairs.

"Tea or coffee?"

"Coffee, please – and one of those biscuits if the boys left any for us!" Ann settled back in her chair.

Kate fetched a half-empty packet from the cupboard. "I always keep some back," she laughed. "They're like gannets when the biscuits appear."

Sitting opposite across the table, they instinctively leant towards each other as Ann prompted Kate to explain. "Tell me more about this conversation with the husband – Michael did you say his name was? And what you wanted from him."

"Michael Bryant." Kate paused. "Well, I remembered last year, when I told Trevor about this child, he said it was so unfair that I could see my – not sure what he called James, probably he just said 'James' – when he didn't know his child. I suppose in a way it is unfair. So, maybe it's daft, but I thought that if they could meet, it might help."

"But wouldn't he want more than just to see him? Wouldn't he want a relationship with him or her, like you have with James?"

Kate looked embarrassed. "To be honest, I hadn't thought beyond a meeting."

Ann looked sceptical. "That was a bit short-sighted. How's Trevor going to feel faced with Nicola? Would you just spring it on him? And what on earth would you say to the boys if he did want a relationship? But for now, tell me, how did you contact this Michael?"

Kate's deepening embarrassment turned to sheepishness. "I got Virginia – Trevor's secretary – to ask HR, said we wanted to welcome Nicola and him to Bristol as she used to work for Trevor at Capital. I had to hide a smile when she said how thoughtful of us! She rang back with his mobile number and his address." Kate went on to relate how she had driven there and been surprised he lived in a modest block of flats. "I explained it to myself by guessing he had moved to Bristol first to look for somewhere suitable for the family."

"Hmm, that's logical. But then what?"

"I called him at the office this afternoon. He was quite friendly to start with, sounded nice. But I got into a real tangle trying to say we wanted to ask him and Nicola to come for a welcome to Bristol drink. When I did manage to be coherent, he turned cold and refused very firmly. I persisted – he must have thought me very rude. Finally, he said there was no point as Nicola had left him to join the father of her child – his exact words. I just burst into tears. God knows what he must have thought of me."

"I'm surprised he didn't just hang up on you – though I suppose he knew you were the managing director's wife, so he had to be polite."

"I got a grip on myself and said I wanted to meet him anyway to talk about – things. I was very persistent, and he finally agreed and said tomorrow evening. Which is why I need a babysitter."

"This takes a bit of digesting." Ann's brow was furrowed. "You really were out of order. Poor man. But what do you hope to get from meeting him?"

"To be honest, I'm not really sure, but I suppose to understand their history together, understand this ghastly situation."

Ann reached across the table and took Kate's hands in hers. "You've jumped to a huge conclusion. There's one big, big question behind all this. When did Nicola leave him? Just recently or months ago? There's no point in making yourself sick if it's not Trevor she's gone back to."

Kate sighed. "Of course you're right. Maybe I really have got the wrong idea. But when he said she had gone back to the father, my world just collapsed. Idiotic, I know, but..."

"Thinking about it, perhaps it is good that you're seeing him. At least you should get the big question answered. What will you do if you find it's not Trevor she's gone to? Just apologise and say goodbye?"

"I think I shall have to do more than just apologise – grovel is more like it. I shall feel a total fool." Kate shook her head as if to clear the thought. "But, heavens, what a relief it would be – worth being a fool for! About babysitting, do you think you could manage? Trevor will be calling six-ish, then I'd give the boys their supper and get them ready for bed and go to his place about eight, I think. It's not far, and I don't imagine it would take long."

"I rang John before I left and he will be in, and I don't think he'll mind if I've got his and the boys' supper ready and I won't be late, so yes – but I expect the full story the minute you get back!" Ann looked Kate in the eye and grinned.

Kate went round the table and gave Ann a hug. "You're a star, and the best friend anyone could wish for."

Ann laughed. "In return, I do get the vicarious thrill of your love life! But now I must tear Mike and Peter away. I expect they've got a bit of homework to do, even if it's just reading."

The boys were called down, farewells were exchanged and Ann drove off, waving as she turned out of the drive.

"OK, you three, have you got any work this evening?"

Heads were shaken happily. "Can we go and play in the garden until supper?"

"Yes, off you go. I'll call you in when Daddy rings." Kate watched as they raced out and started a game of cricket using an upturned bucket as the wicket. The ball frequently disappeared into the rose bed, but she didn't go out to remonstrate. Turning back, she picked up her phone and sent a short text to Michael Bryant: *Got a babysitter. See you about 8.15 tomorrow. OK?*

Her phone pinged with the reply almost immediately. *OK. Coffee?*

She suddenly realised he might have thought she expected dinner, so this was a relief. She texted back. *Fine, thanks. See you tomorrow.*

Chapter 37

Kate managed to speak calmly when Trevor called that evening, briefly asking after his day and mentioning that Ann had brought her two sons round to play after school. She passed the phone to the boys, who hogged the line with the tale of the impromptu cricket match.

"The ball kept going in the rose bed, but we were really careful getting it out – those roses have horrible thorns!"

Kate could hear Trevor's laughing response. "Next time, have the wicket at the other end of the garden – you'll be much safer and so will the roses!"

"Same time tomorrow?" Kate asked him as the boys finished, crossing her fingers that it wouldn't be any later.

"I think so. Bye, love you."

"Bye," shouted all three boys, drowning out Kate's "I love you."

The evening was interrupted by Trevor calling again.

"I forgot to say, I should get into Bristol around ten on Friday evening. I'll get a taxi home."

"Thanks, darling. Do you think you'll want anything to eat when you get in?"

"No, there'll be snacks on the plane, and anyway I'll be pretty knackered as it'll have been a long day."

"OK, see you Friday – I'll probably be asleep if you're delayed but don't worry, no need to creep in."

Trevor laughed. "I shall wake you with a kiss, like Prince Charming. OK?"

"Very OK! Bye." Kate blew a kiss down the line and closed the call.

Next day, Kate was very glad she had her morning duty at the charity shop to take her mind off the evening ahead. The rest of the day she tried to concentrate on domestic chores and giving the boys attention after school.

That evening's call from Trevor was very brief. "Sorry, can't talk, got a business dinner and still got some work to do before it. Everything OK with you?"

"Yes, fine. We'll catch up at the weekend. Looking forward to having you back – the bed is awfully big for one! See you tomorrow night. Big kiss." Kate was very relieved not to have to have a longer conversation when she was so nervous about meeting Michael Bryant, but couldn't stop herself momentarily wondering whether the business dinner was with Nicola. Stop it! she admonished herself.

Ann arrived as the boys finished their baths and were ready for bedtime reading.

"I'm happy to read to James – and the others if they want. You go and change and get this meeting over with – and remember, I shall want a full account!" Ann smiled, but her face showed her concern at how difficult the meeting was likely to be.

Kate went upstairs to change. She decided against putting on mascara in case she once again started to cry, though she instructed herself to remain cool, calm and collected. Some hope, she admitted as she went to kiss the boys good night.

The traffic was very light and it took only ten minutes to reach the flats and park in the area under the arch. Glancing at her watch, she saw it was 8.20 – perfect, she thought, not too prompt, but not late either.

The butterflies were back with a vengeance as she rang the bell and announced herself over the intercom.

"First floor," the disembodied voice announced.

The door buzzed. Kate pushed it open and went into an entry hall devoid of pictures but clean and tidy. She forced herself to breathe normally as she climbed the stairs.

The door to Flat 4 opened as she approached. The man facing her was much older than she had envisaged – at least fifty, grey-haired and with a slight paunch. Taken aback, she was momentarily silent. Quickly recovering herself, she held out her hand, hoping he hadn't noticed.

"Michael Bryant? I'm Kate Martin. Thank you so much for agreeing to meet."

"Come in," he said without a smile, pointing to the main room. "Please take a seat while I make the coffee." He disappeared into the kitchen.

Kate chose one of the two armchairs in front of a fireplace with a fake fire partly hidden behind a large bowl of hydrangeas. She surveyed the spacious but simply-furnished room, book-laden shelves, a large flat-screen TV in one corner.

She rose as Michael Bryant returned carrying a tray with two mugs of coffee, milk jug and sugar bowl which he set down on a small table between the armchairs.

"Milk and sugar?"

"Neither, thanks, I'll take it black." She held out her hand to receive the mug and was pleased to find it was strong fresh coffee. "Thank you." She sat down again.

Her host sat down in the other armchair, cradling his coffee in both hands.

"Well, Mrs Martin, why are you here?"

All day she had been practising in her head how to approach the subject. But faced with the immediate need to explain, Kate suddenly found herself tongue-tied. She played for time, taking a sip of coffee and pronouncing it good. Take a grip, she told herself, and tried a tentative smile.

"Yesterday," she began, "I rang to invite you and Nicola round for a drink to welcome you both to Bristol and Staffords. You declined, then reluctantly said it was because Nicola had left to join the father of her son so there was no point. I burst into tears. I'll try to explain why, but first, please, tell me: when did she leave you?" Kate held her breath.

"What an odd question. Three months ago."

At this, Kate didn't know whether to laugh or, once again, burst into tears – though this time they would be tears of relief. However, she managed to restrain herself.

"You can't imagine how relieved I am by that. I had stupidly jumped to the wrong conclusion." Kate smiled at him happily. "But although it's a huge relief to me, I'm very sorry for you as, from the way you told me on the phone that she had left, you were clearly very hurt."

"Yes, I was."

"Look, Michael – may we please call each other Michael and Kate? Mr and Mrs is just too formal for this strange conversation." Kate looked at him enquiringly.

He nodded but said nothing.

Kate realised this evening was going to be even more of a strain than she had anticipated but persevered, her curiosity getting the better of her. "Had you been married long?"

"Look, before we go any further, Kate – please tell me what's behind this. You owe me that."

Kate opened her mouth to answer, to tell him about Trevor and Nicola, but suddenly realised what she was about to reveal about the managing director of Staffords to one of his staff. And what would Trevor say when he discovered she had told their story, not just to a stranger but to a colleague? She cringed inwardly but knew she had to carry on – it was that or turn and leave immediately which would not only be very rude, but leave open the festering sore, perhaps for both of them.

"Please, please treat this in strictest confidence; I would be devastated if the story got around. A few years ago – six or seven, actually – my husband –" She paused, suddenly realising she had been so focused on Trevor and Nicola that she hadn't stopped to think she would be talking about the wife of the man in front of her – the man whom Nicola had badly hurt.

"Oh, God. I'm sorry, Michael, I've got myself into very deep water. If I tell you the whole story, it's likely to upset you as much as it has upset me."

Michael looked her in the eye. "I need to know everything. I don't think you can hurt me any more than Nicola has already. I was seriously taken in by her." He paused. "And I promise you faithfully that not a word of this will go beyond this room. I wouldn't dream of saying anything to your husband – not that our paths are likely to cross."

"Thank you." Kate felt instinctively she could trust him on this and began.

"Trevor still worked for Capital then and Nicola was his legal assistant. I discovered they were having an affair. I kept quiet, thinking office romances usually died of their own accord, but later it nearly broke our marriage." Kate found having to speak across the considerable distance between the chairs rather intimidating.

She continued, quickly deciding to keep James out of the story as much as she could. As well as protecting herself, it didn't directly impinge on Nicola.

"We had a third son, and last spring when James was about five, Trevor became very cold, distant and difficult. When I finally confronted him, he got very angry, said he wanted a divorce because –" She hesitated. "Because he thought I was seeing someone. I wasn't, he had completely misread something. Anyway, we had a massive row and at that point I told him I had known about the affair. He was shocked – and embarrassed – that I knew but hadn't said anything. But then he told me the whole history – how Nicola had set her cap at him, deliberately standing too close, letting their hands touch accidentally, and making it clear she fancied him.

"He's only human, and when they were on a business trip to Germany together and drank rather too much wine over dinner, the inevitable happened. Trevor said that Nicola had kept pressuring him to leave me and marry her but by then I was pregnant with James and he had flatly refused. He insisted it had just been an office romance, as I had hoped, and he had never had any intention of leaving me.

"He managed to get Nicola transferred to head office in London with a higher salary, and he moved to Staffords. I should add that, apart from around the time of the showdown, we had a very good marriage and fundamentally neither of us wanted to break it – it was awful that we got so near the brink."

Michael nodded but said nothing.

Kate sighed. "But then we come to the twist – the one which has brought me here. A former colleague of Trevor's at Capital told us that Nicola had had a child who was about the same age as our James. Trevor immediately assumed he was the father. I discovered very recently that he had become obsessed with this child and had been lying to me about working late on business trips to London. He was so desperate to see the child – he had decided it was a boy – that he had actually been spending the evenings trying to track you and Nicola down." She shook her head in bewilderment at the lengths to which Trevor had gone. "We had another almighty row, and I… I really did think about leaving him. But we somehow got through it."

Her voice faltered as she recounted the final part of the story, reliving her phone call with Michael. "Trevor went to Germany on business again this week. When you said Nicola had left you to join the father of her child, my world just collapsed – and that's why I burst into tears on the phone. I know I stupidly jumped to conclusions, but I think you understand now why I needed to talk to you and why my first question was, when did she leave you?" She looked down again, embarrassed.

They were both silent for a few moments, avoiding each other's eyes. Michael was the first to break the silence.

"I'm really sorry, that was brave of you. I can see you've been as damaged by Nicola as I have. But you've added to my understanding of her, and it's not a good revelation. I think I should tell you about my relationship with her – and how your husband can't be the father." He sat back in his chair and closed his eyes.

Kate could sense him gathering the strength to share what were obviously very painful memories.

He opened his eyes and leant forward, his gaze not on her but on the bowl of hydrangeas.

"It began about six years ago..."

Chapter 38

Michael began very slowly. "When Nicola was transferred to London, she was assigned to my department, Litigation, and I was asked to mentor her. She was very bright but somehow managed to need a lot of attention. She was chatty, and over coffee we talked about ourselves. She soon learnt that my first wife had died five years earlier and that to our great sadness we had been unable to have children."

Michael paused, then looked up at Kate.

"It will help you to understand if you know I'm the only child of elderly academic parents. I'd always dreamt of having children to give them the childhood I would have loved. Nicola seemed very sympathetic. She became almost over-friendly – just as you described with Trevor – coming very close, letting our hands touch, making me feel special.

"I can't deny I found her very attractive, and I was lonely, still missing my wife and had no female friends, let alone girlfriends. So you shouldn't be surprised that I soon found myself in love with her. I didn't say anything directly to her, thinking she wouldn't see me in that way as I was quite a bit older than her, but she must have guessed.

"Anyway, one morning she came into my office and burst into tears. Instinctively, I took her in my arms to comfort her. It didn't take much persuading to get her to tell me what was wrong. She said she had discovered a few weeks before that her boyfriend, who had promised to marry her, was already married and had gone back to his wife. And now she had found she was pregnant and didn't know what to do.

"Impulsively, I asked her to marry me, confessed I loved her and said I would look after her and the child. She was so sweet, said it was a wonderful idea and would give me the child – maybe even children – that I had always wanted, and that she would grow to love me as I was such a special person."

Michael's voice faltered. He fished in his pocket for a handkerchief, and Kate saw his eyes were now wet with tears. Her instinct was to reach across to comfort him, but she sat still.

"Can you go on, or is it too hard?"

"I must go on." Michael spoke more strongly. "I've never told anyone this story. It's a relief to share it at last – especially with you who, I believe, will understand the pain it's caused me."

"So, did you get married straight away?" Kate hoped her interjection would help him.

"Pretty much, but very quietly, and we only told close colleagues; I could hardly have kept it secret. To begin with, it all went really well. I was so happy – I loved seeing her belly swell, anticipating being a father at last. Nicola was a delight to be with – attentive, loving even. Then the baby – a boy – was born. I have to confess that I was disconcerted when I first saw him, though I was ashamed of my reaction and did my best to hide it."

"Why?" Kate couldn't stop herself from interrupting.

"He was pretty obviously mixed-race."

Kate gasped, but she stifled her questions, allowing Michael to continue in his own way.

"But he was very beautiful, exquisite, and as soon as I was allowed to hold him, my heart was completely won. Nicola was lovely with him, and I truly believed we were destined to be a happy family. It was only as he got older and began to talk that Nicola started to withdraw from me. She went back to work part time, and he went to nursery. She did let me share the parenting, though, and I developed a really strong relationship with him."

"What did you call him?"

"David. David Christopher Olongo Bryant. The middle names must be from the father. I really wanted him to be David Michael, but Nicola refused point-blank. That hurt."

"I can imagine." Kate paused before asking, "Did Nicola ever talk about the father? He obviously still mattered to her if she called her son after him."

"No. If I ever tried to ask about him, she more or less told me to shut up. It was strange; you would have thought she would want to vent her anger and disappointment. Perhaps I should have been suspicious..." Michael's voice tailed off.

"So, when did you realise that he was still part of her life? Did she give any hints as to her intention to leave?"

"No, none. It was entirely out of the blue. One day I came home from work expecting Nicola to have collected David from school, be giving him his supper as usual, but..." Michael swallowed before continuing, talking faster as if to get the tale over and done with. "But the house was empty – it had that feel when you know no-one's there. I went into David's room. Everything was perfectly neat, but I saw an envelope on his bed. I somehow knew it was bad news, my hands were shaking. The letter said simply, *Christopher's divorce through. Gone with David to join him in Nigeria. Divorce me*." At this point Michael, all restraint gone, wept openly, his head in his hands.

Kate could stay seated no longer. She stood, went over to Michael and put her hand on his shoulder.

"I'm sorry, Michael. I'm so, so sorry."

Michael acknowledged her sympathy with a nod, wiped his wet cheeks with his handkerchief and sat up straight, visibly fighting to regain control. Kate sat down again, and there was silence for a few minutes. Kate was the first to speak.

"It's unbelievable. So callous, so cruel." She paused, then continued tentatively, "Do you think her wooing – no, entrapment is a better word – of you follows from her failure to get Trevor?"

Michael looked at her directly. "I've a feeling you might be right."

"It beggars belief that she could be so calculating." Kate shook her head in mystification. "Can you think what her motivation was, what was driving such incredible behaviour?"

"I don't think that's difficult," said Michael ruefully. "I'm guessing she knew this Christopher was married all along and didn't quite believe in the promised divorce. She hedged her bets by chatting up other men she thought might marry her. That would be when the Trevor phase began. Then she found she was pregnant and put pressure on Trevor to marry her – from what you've said, I don't think she told him she was pregnant – but he refused to leave you and sent her away. She couldn't face single motherhood and Christopher maybe reneging on his promise, so she looked around to find someone she could seduce who would look after her and the baby." Michael sighed. "And I was the mug – single, lonely, vulnerable. The fact that I had told her about my longing to have children made it easy for her to admit her pregnancy and give me the sob story – which was, in fact, half true."

Kate nodded agreement. "That makes sense. But you said she was really nice to you at first, you were happy. Then she went cold. What do you think changed?"

"I can't know for sure, but I would guess she was in contact with Christopher all along and at some point he must have started divorce proceedings which gave her hope, and he kept her up to date with how things were going, so she could plan to leave me."

"Still, the way she left – without a word of warning, no hint to you of her plans. I find that unforgivable. And the devastation of losing David… How you must have felt when you found they had gone and just that curt note on David's bed." Kate felt a wave of sympathy as she imagined that moment.

Abruptly, Michael stood up. "I think we need something stronger than coffee after that. Will you have a brandy or maybe a glass of wine before you go?"

Kate looked at her watch and was surprised to see it was only 9.15.

"Yes, please, a brandy would be great. But just a small one, as I'm driving, and I promised my friend who's babysitting that I'd be back by ten."

While Michael was fetching glasses and the brandy from the kitchen, Kate got up and walked round the room, pausing in front of the bookshelves where three photographs in silver frames stood on one shelf. Seeing they were all of a small boy at different ages, without thinking she picked up one to look more closely.

Just then, Michael returned, a glass of brandy in each hand. Embarrassed, Kate moved to put the photo back, but Michael came and stood beside her.

"I like to look at them every day," he said with a smile, half sad, half proud, handing her one of the glasses.

"I can understand that." Kate looked at the three photos. "He really is a beautiful child, such lovely colouring – and his eyes! They shine with intelligence."

"Thank you. And yes, he is very intelligent. I loved talking to him, explaining things, introducing him to new ideas." Michael looked away. "How I miss him."

Kate, unable to think quickly of a response that was not trite or mawkish, returned the photo to its place with a smile, and they went back to their seats.

"Cheers," Michael raised his glass.

"Cheers," Kate responded. "But that doesn't seem appropriate." She paused a moment. "I salute a kind man who has been badly treated and hope that the wound, deep though it is, will heal in time."

"Thank you. And thank you for forcing this meeting. Hard though it was, it has been really helpful – cathartic, in a way – to share the story."

They sipped the brandy in silence, avoiding each other's eyes, both deep in thought. Kate then looked up.

"How on earth am I going to break the news to Trevor? If I tell him I rang you at the office then came to meet you here, he will think I've been snooping, going behind his back – which is true. And when he does learn the truth, that he was not the father after all, he will feel even more foolish than he does already." Kate stopped there, remembering that Michael didn't know of Trevor's humiliation at the hands of the police.

"I doubt I can help." Michael smiled kindly at her. "I'm afraid that's your problem."

Kate nodded and stood up to go.

"Thank you again for talking to me – I think you understand how important it was for me and how grateful I am."

"You know my number, so you can call me if needed." He held out his hand. Kate shook it warmly then turned to the door. "Good night – and good luck."

"Good night." The door closed behind her. She returned to her car, her mind racing, and drove home.

Chapter 39

Kate paused before getting out of the car. Her head had been reeling with the emotions aroused by her evening with Michael Bryant, and now she had to decide how much to tell Ann. Would it be fair to reveal Michael's traumatic experience? She was still thinking when the front door opened revealing Ann looking both worried and questioning.

"Hi, I heard the car." Unable to conceal her impatient curiosity, she stepped out and embraced Kate as she emerged from the car, then, an arm around Kate's waist, led her to the house. "Tell all!"

"Let's sit down first – give me a moment to calm down." Kate moved to the kitchen, scene of previous confidence sharing. She sat, leaning back in her chair, facing Ann.

"Well?"

"Before I begin, this is in total confidence. Michael and I swore his story would go no further, so you mustn't even tell John."

"I promise." Ann made as if to do a Scout's Honour gesture but, quickly realising it wasn't a joking matter, settled instead for repeating, "I promise."

Kate continued. "Honestly, it was strange, really forced at first, as you can imagine – remember, he'd been very reluctant to meet me."

Ann nodded.

"I couldn't hold back, though, and asked him straight out when Nicola had left him. He hesitated, but I think he could see how important it was to me and said three months ago. You can guess I was almost ecstatic with relief that she hadn't gone to join Trevor. I didn't know whether to laugh or cry."

"My God, that is a relief." Ann paused, a worried frown creasing her forehead. "But couldn't she have left and joined Trevor later?"

"I didn't think of that then, fortunately. Anyway, I explained why his answer had been so important to me, and as I described the Nicola and Trevor business, he became very attentive and then told me everything." Kate summarised what Michael had revealed. "Poor man. Nicola realised he was lonely and vulnerable – his words. He fell in love with her, she gave him a big sob story about how she was pregnant and her boyfriend had abandoned her, and he offered to marry her…"

Ann interrupted, "Pregnant with Trevor's child? Heavens…"

"No, not Trevor's child, thank God." Kate savoured the revelation she was about to make. "Apparently, the marriage was happy to begin with – at least from Michael's point of view – and when the baby was born, it was clear he was mixed-race!"

Ann's eyebrows shot up, and a quiet 'phew' escaped her lips.

Kate smiled. "I saw photos of him – a gorgeous child. Though it was a surprise to Michael, it wasn't a problem. He got very attached to the boy, David, who's about the same age as our James, was a real father to him. But three months ago, Nicola left, totally without warning. Just left a note saying she'd gone to join the boyfriend in Nigeria taking David with her – no details – and to divorce her."

"I can hardly believe it. Poor man." Ann shook her head. "What a sad story. So, do you think she fixed on Michael when Trevor refused to marry her?"

"Looks like it. And I think she had always planned to leave him, was just waiting for the word from the boyfriend. She'd insisted the baby be David Christopher Olongo, so it confirms the boyfriend was very probably Nigerian."

Both women sat in silence for a minute. Then Kate ventured, "Now I've got to break the news to Trevor that he's wasted huge amounts of time and emotional energy trying to see his supposed son. I don't know how to do it without letting on I've been snooping behind his back – I don't want him to feel foolish."

"No, I can see it's not going to be a comfortable revelation. Oh, dear." Ann sighed. "But you mustn't put it off."

"No, you're right. He'll be home tomorrow night, so I don't have much time to think."

Ann looked at her watch. "Sorry, I really must go home now – John will be waiting up for me." She stood up. "Thanks for telling me, well done for being brave enough to force the meeting with Michael Bryant, and good luck with Trevor. And you know I'm always here if you need to talk."

"No, I must thank you for listening – and for babysitting this evening. Just imagine if I'd had to go on wondering if Trevor was with Nicola. It doesn't bear thinking about." Kate gave Ann a big hug and went with her to the front door. "Bye, and love and thanks to John – but don't tell him any of this. You promised."

Kate made her way wearily up to bed, stopping to check on the boys who, she was relieved to see, were all fast asleep. She was in bed and hoping sleep would come quickly when a rush of heat ran through her as she suddenly understood that she was indeed, albeit unintentionally, the cause of Trevor's obsession.

Abruptly she sat up, beating her head with her hands as she castigated herself aloud. "How could I have been so focused on Trevor's obsession without understanding what gave rise to it, that he was right, it is partly my fault." She sat a few minutes longer, running through that horrible first row when he had demanded a divorce, and she had told him about Nicola's child with the intention of making him understand they were both at fault. She had assumed that Trevor was the father and had certainly meant him to believe it.

"But it was a perfectly reasonable assumption," she said, again out loud, allowing herself a modicum of forgiveness. "After all, the child and James were about the same age."

Lying down again, she curled up under the duvet, knowing that her sleep would be troubled by this new sense of guilt, while at the same time hoping it might help her in admitting her Michael Bryant visit to Trevor.

Chapter 40

Trevor looked at his watch as the taxi drew up outside the house on Friday evening. Well past eleven, Kate would probably be asleep. He paid, shut the cab door quietly and walked up the drive. He still got a shiver of shock and shame as he remembered the accident and Kate discovering his lies. What a ghastly few days that had been, but thank God James had recovered so well and Kate had allowed herself to be won back. It was all so vivid it could have been yesterday, rather than a few weeks ago.

He let himself into the house, taking care not to let the door slam. The bedroom door was slightly ajar but the room was dark except for the dim square of light from the street lamps penetrating the curtains. He put his bag down and crept in as silently as he could. Once inside, he could see Kate curled on one side, her book face down on the pillow. Not sure if he was pleased not to have disturbed her, or disappointed that she wasn't awake to welcome him, he began to undress.

"So, where's the prince who was going to wake me with a kiss?"

Trevor laughed, bent down and kissed first the top of her head, then as she turned slightly, he gave the returning-to-life kiss he had promised.

Kate sat up and switched on the bedside light. "Hi, darling, how was Germany?"

"It went very well." Trevor sat down on the bed. "The good news is that I won't have to spend as much time there as I thought."

"What's the bad news?"

"There isn't any!" Trevor kissed her lightly again. "Actually, there's more good news. We'll have that Cape Cod holiday as planned, plus…" He paused for effect. "Plus, the company wants me to go to the States about then anyway, and they've said they'll pay the fares for all of us as a sort of bonus!"

"Wow, that's brilliant, really generous – and a compliment to you. We'll be able to do all the fun things on offer without worrying about our budget." Kate smiled happily. "But right now, come to bed – the boys are so keen to have you back, they're bound to come in early."

Trevor complied and was soon stretched out beside Kate. He pulled her gently into an embrace. "I think we should risk the early awakening. I know I was only away a few days, but I missed you so much."

Their love-making was brief but intensely satisfying, and sleep came quickly, at least for Trevor, unaware of Kate's restless rehearsal of the news she planned to impart next day.

******

The morning broke grey and windy. Kate and Trevor were roused by the boys bouncing on their bed.

"Hi, Dad, it's really windy. Can we fly the kites again?"

"No, let's go to see Nana and Pops."

"I want to go to the zoo!"

"Hold on, hold on! It's only half past seven." Trevor roused himself with difficulty. "Give your poor Dad a chance. Let's have breakfast first, and then we can plan the day."

Somehow, the day's activities were organised to everyone's satisfaction. Both Kate and Trevor managed calls to their respective parents, Kate able to tell hers the good news about the Cape Cod holiday, and Trevor his that the day out with them had been such a success that James was jealous he had missed it. It was happily agreed another outing would be arranged in the school holidays.

Trevor noticed that at times Kate seemed a little withdrawn but was too engaged with the boys to question it. As the boys were enjoying their baths after playtime and supper, however, he took advantage of the temporary lull.

"Everything OK, darling? You seem a bit preoccupied."

"No, I'm fine, but there is something I need to tell you. Maybe after dinner." Kate managed a reassuring smile.

Trevor looked at her questioningly, but she had turned away to get clean towels from the airing cupboard. His first thought – to his surprise – was whether she might be pregnant and realised he wasn't sure how he would feel about that. Then that there was a problem with one of the children at school, or... His heart lurched. Surely nothing to do with Jonathan Markham and James. His attention was brought back to the present as Kate returned with the towels and asked him to get the boys into bed and stories read while she finished preparing their dinner.

It was with some trepidation that he joined Kate at the table. He was pleased that she had put out a good bottle of wine to go with the chicken casserole.

"Thank you, darling, delicious. It's so good to be back. As I've said before, hotel food just isn't the same." He poured them each a glass and raised his in a toast. "Here's to home, a wonderful family, and a great holiday to look forward to."

Kate raised hers and echoed his sentiment, but more simply. "Here's to us."

Trevor was momentarily reassured but still found it hard to avoid questioning Kate as they ate. Fresh fruit salad and biscuits and cheese completed the meal. To his slight surprise, Kate suggested they finish the wine and have their coffee in the kitchen.

"It's cosier, less formal." Kate looked at him. "I said I had something to tell you – I think now is the moment, and I don't want it to be like our last two confrontations."

Trevor flinched inwardly and braced himself for some new revelation. He was surprised by Kate's opening sentence.

"I've been feeling really bad about the Nicola's child thing, the embarrassment and misery you went through, as I've come to realise it really was largely my fault – even though I slapped you when you said that in the hospital."

Trevor opened his mouth to demur, but Kate held up her hand to stop him.

"When we had that first row a year ago, you accused me of having an affair with Jonathan Markham. I admitted Jonathan was James's father as you had guessed, but then I told you I knew about your affair with Nicola and that I had discovered she had a child about the same age as James. I told you because I wanted you to understand that we had both behaved appallingly. I didn't actually say it was your child, though it was the obvious inference, but I certainly encouraged you to come to that conclusion." Kate had been unable to look at Trevor as she spoke, but now she raised her eyes to meet his as she continued. "And you did come round, forgave me. Then you said something about how it was unfair that I could see James all the time, but you didn't know anything about your child by Nicola. Remember?"

Trevor nodded, wondering what exactly was coming next but very aware that it would have to do with his efforts to see the child.

"Well, when the stalking incident happened and I discovered the lengths you went to, the lies you had told me, it was quite a shock. You really did almost break our marriage then. But thank heavens for your romantic streak. It would have taken a far tougher woman than me to resist that letter and the promise of all those roses on every anniversary." At this point Kate smiled at him.

A grin lit Trevor's previously anxious face. "I can't tell you how relieved I was – am – that you're not tougher! My heart was in my mouth until you rang and said you would come home."

"Well, I'm afraid you're going to be very angry with me now, because once I realised just how important seeing the child was to you, I began to think about what I could do, how I could possibly engineer it."

Now Trevor was all attention. The surroundings – the table, glasses, cheese – became a blur; his focus was entirely on Kate as he hardly dared think what was coming.

Kate took a deep breath. "I checked with Virginia that Michael Bryant had started work at Staffords, and I rang him at the office and invited him and Nicola here for a welcome to Bristol drink."

"You did WHAT?" Trevor could hardly believe his ears. "Without telling me!"

"Yes, I did. And I'm not sorry." Kate was defiant. "I thought that, since their child and James are the same age, it could be a way of..."

"Stop. I can't believe you did this." Trevor thumped the table, making the glasses jump. "How do you think I would feel being forced to be nice to Nicola, never mind her husband – we don't know whether he knows about me. God, how embarrassing."

"I knew I had to take that risk, or you might go on wondering about your child and getting into goodness knows what trouble, even though you said you would stop. Anyway, it's done, but not without causing me a terrible 24 hours."

"Go on."

"Michael was..."

"Oh, so it's Michael now, is it?" Trevor felt a knife was twisting his gut.

Kate ignored him.

"Michael was very cold and unfriendly, turned the invitation down flat." A fleeting look of relief passed over Trevor's face, but Kate continued as if he had not reacted. "I pressed him for a reason, and he said it was because Nicola had left him to join the father of her child. Given that you were away, I jumped to the conclusion that she had gone to join you. Imagine how I felt."

"How on earth can you have thought that, given what we'd been through recently – and the roses. Would I have said all that if I was about to leave you? Honestly…" Trevor blustered.

"But remember how many times you've lied to me before. Could I really, really trust you, however much I wanted to?"

Trevor had the grace to look a little ashamed.

"Anyway, I burst into tears on the phone. Michael softened a bit at that. I was desperate to know the truth, and I persuaded him to meet me – so I went to his flat last night." Trevor looked like thunder, but Kate continued, warning him with a look not to interrupt. "Calm down, it was all very proper. Ann babysat for me – I told her where and why I was going, so it wasn't secret."

"My God, Kate, you mean you've been telling Ann about – about us? Who else have you been blabbing to? This is worse and worse."

"Stop it. That's a mean response when you've caused me such misery over the past year." Kate's voice left no doubt of her feelings. "The day after the stalking and James's accident, I broke down when Ann phoned, and she came over to find out what was wrong. I told her. I couldn't keep it back. You have to believe me, she's the only person who knows, and she's been a brick."

"OK, I believe you," Trevor agreed reluctantly but was impatient to know more. "So, what happened with Michael Bryant?"

"Almost as soon as I arrived, I asked him outright when Nicola had left. He said three months ago. It shouldn't take much imagination for you to realise what an extraordinary relief that was."

"You should have trusted me…"

Kate didn't bother replying but continued with, "He told me the whole story of his relationship with Nicola. Sadly for him, she seduced him after you had refused to marry her and got her transferred to London. She told him she was pregnant but the father had dumped her. By then Michael had fallen in love with her and offered to marry her. Poor man, it was an awful mistake. You had a very narrow escape."

"What do you mean, why a narrow escape?"

"Well, when she left him, she went without any warning. Michael got home from work one day, found the house empty and a note on the boy's bed. The note read, 'Gone with David to join Christopher in Nigeria. Divorce me.' Then he understood that not only was the father definitely Nigerian, but that child, the son he had grown to love deeply and been a true father to, would be living so far away."

Trevor's face was a picture – shock, embarrassment and relief mingling.

"So, I'm not the father?"

"No, you're not." Kate reached over the table and took Trevor's hand in hers. "Now you understand why I feel so guilty, as I planted the idea in the first place. I'm truly, truly sorry. I've caused you so much misery this past year. Can you forgive me?"

Trevor was silent, eyes downcast. Eventually he looked up and Kate could see tears forming. She held his hand more tightly and after a few moments, ventured to speak.

"Please, can you – will you forgive me? I love you and hate the mess we – I – got us into."

Trevor couldn't hold back the tears. He pulled his hand from hers and fished for a handkerchief. "Oh, Kate, dearest Kate. What I put you through doesn't bear thinking about. Of course I forgive you." Putting down the handkerchief, he reached for Kate's hand again.

"More importantly, can you forgive me? I was the one who had the affair which started this whole sorry saga."

Kate relinquished his hand and came to his side of the table. Standing behind his chair, she put her arms round him, kissed the top of his head and whispered in his ear.

“It’s over, we’re starting again with a fabulous holiday to look forward to. We can put all this behind us.” Pulling him gently from his chair, she led him towards the stairs, leaving the remains of the meal on the table which had been witness to the end of a sad and difficult year.

As he followed Kate, full of regret at the traumas of the past year and happy that the nightmare was over, at every step a refrain ran through Trevor’s head:

Not my child.

Not my child.

Not my child.

Acknowledgements

Huge thanks to the indomitable, inspiring Maggie Smith, who convened a small group of writers, all of us embarking on a novel. We – Maggie, Tony Emerson, Patsy Way and Pia Helena Ormerod – met every two or three weeks, over more than two years, to offer each other constructive insights and encouragement. Without them, this book would never have seen the light of day.

Thanks, too, to Dave Firth for proofreading, to Robyn Smith for the cover design, and to my husband, Oliver, who never normally reads novels but said he enjoyed this one!

About the Author

Having studied Natural Sciences at Cambridge, Sue worked as a financial analyst before marrying and having two sons. The family lived in Montreal for three years and in Switzerland for seven before settling back in London where, with her husband, she bought and expanded a small estate agency. Following the sale of the agency, Sue became very involved in the not-for-profit sector, as a supporter, volunteer and as chair of several charities. With her husband she has travelled very widely, enjoying the different cultures around the world, including in some very out-of-the-way places.

Lightning Source UK Ltd.
Milton Keynes UK
UKHW012244051021
391692UK00001B/15

9 781803 021850